SEA CHASE

SEA CHASE

Curtis Parkinson (signature)

CURTIS PARKINSON

Tundra Books

Published in Canada by Tundra Books,
481 University Avenue, Toronto, Ontario M5G 2E9

Published in the United States by Tundra Books of Northern New York,
P.O. Box 1030, Plattsburgh, New York 12901

Library of Congress Control Number: 2004100579

National Library of Canada Cataloguing in Publication

Parkinson, Curtis
        Sea chase / Curtis Parkinson.

For ages 10-14.
ISBN 0-88776-682-X

        I. Title.

PS8581.A76234S42 2004   JC813'.54   C2004-900496-4

We acknowledge the financial support of the Government of Canada
through the Book Publishing Industry Development Program (BPIDP)
and that of the Government of Ontario through the Ontario Media
Development Corporation's Ontario Book Initiative. We further
acknowledge the support of the Canada Council for the Arts and the
Ontario Arts Council for our publishing program.

Design: Terri Nimmo

Printed and bound in Canada

This book is printed on acid-free paper that is 100% recycled,
ancient-forest friendly (40 % post-consumer recycled).

1 2 3 4 5 6   09 08 07 06 05 04

To the brave people of Colombia

"Youth and Hope – those twin realities of this phantom world."

– Samuel Taylor Coleridge

1

Drifting in and out, in and out, in and out between sleeping and waking, Brodie Bailey came to slowly. He opened one eye and tried to focus on the ship's clock in the dim light. Four thirty.

Couldn't be. He sat up abruptly. Yet it was. *How come?* Why hadn't his father called him at four? A stickler for detail, his father always changed watches on time, right to the minute.

He listened to the *slap-slap-slap* of waves against the hull, the creaking of the boom overhead. He felt the up-and-down motion of *Southern Cross* riding the swells of the western Caribbean. Seemed normal enough. So why hadn't his dad called him?

Four hours on, four hours off – that was their routine. Had been for days now. *How many days? Four, or was it five?* One day blended into another out here.

"I'll take the graveyard shift," his father had said, when they started out. "You take the four to eight." That suited Brodie. While his dad liked the night and the stars,

Brodie preferred the dawn. It was tough getting up at four in the morning, but he loved watching the sky slowly lighten, loved watching the sun peek over the horizon like it was checking out the new day. He would greet it with a wave. "Hey, Sun."

Brodie fell back, closed his eyes, and let the boat rock him, making excuses for not getting up. They were away from the shipping lanes, the trade wind blowing steady, the boat steering herself — maybe his father had decided to let him sleep in for a change.

No, not his father.

Maybe it was a reward for last night when Brodie, studying the southern horizon, had made their very first sighting of the constellation after which *Southern Cross* was named.

Nah, his father didn't give rewards.

Oh well, just enjoy it, Brodie, he told himself. He rolled over, accidentally knocking his journal on the floor. He dusted off the cover where he'd printed THE VOYAGE OF SOUTHERN CROSS. The journal fell open to the first page.

He read a bit aloud to hear how his writing sounded: "After months of preparation, we left Puerto Rico for the Panama Canal — the first leg of my father's dream to sail across the Pacific, and my first time at sea." *Not a bad beginning,* he decided. Feeling around in the bunk, he found his pen and changed "my father's dream" to "my father's plan."

He flipped through, reading bits here and there: "Wind calmer today. Nothing special on watch. Caught up on journal, but forgot to record the knotmeter readings – hell to pay." Then there were dolphin sightings, a scary "blue darter" squall, and a near miss by a charging tanker. Mixed in were comments like: "Messed up trying to tack today. . . . Jib got tangled around forestay. . . . If looks could kill. . . ."

Closing the journal, Brodie tucked it carefully away, under his pillow. He stretched – an unexpected luxury. Usually his dad shook him awake, telling him to hit the deck. *What's holding him up this morning?*

Maybe he'd had to make a repair. Something always needed fixing on a boat, Brodie was learning – a chafed line to be replaced, a complaining block to be lubricated. His father was a stickler about those things too, and he meticulously noted jobs for Brodie on the calendar: grease winches, touch up varnish, tighten all shackles. And if he didn't do them on time, Brodie heard about it.

If he's fixing something now, Brodie thought, *I should be up there helping, or I'll be in trouble. I'd better go see.* He swung his legs to the floor.

With only four hours to sleep, he didn't bother with pajamas. Just climbed into his bunk, clothes and all. Now he slipped into the head and gave his teeth a quick brush, leaving the light off so as not to destroy his night vision. He sat on the toilet to pee, having learned from experience he could miss if he did it standing up and the boat yawed suddenly. Then he pasted a smile on his face and headed for the companionway.

"Hey, Dad," he began as he emerged, "you didn't call –"

He stopped partway up the steps. The cockpit was empty.

The waning moon shone through the spokes of the unattended wheel. He saw the wheel revolve slightly, as if guided by a ghostly hand, which meant, he knew, that the self-steering was in control. He turned, expecting to see his father working somewhere on deck.

He stared, transfixed, at the length of deck and beyond – there was nothing but the white tops of waves lit by the sinking moon. . . .

2

"Him and his grandiose ideas," Brodie's mother had said over the phone. "It'll end in disaster, like all his other schemes. I don't want you going with him, you hear?"

He'd stared out the window of the phone booth at a cruiser pulling into the dock.

"Brodie, are you there?"

"Yes."

"Did you hear what I said?"

"It's not a very good connection."

"I said you're not to go with him. You'll miss another year of school."

"What do you mean, *another* year? I've hardly missed any yet, Mom."

"But what are the schools like down there? Did you learn anything?"

"They're okay, and I can speak Spanish now."

"Street Spanish, I'll bet. Look, Brodie, you come back here and finish high school. Then you'll be ready to go on to college."

The sun beat into the booth. With the door closed, it was heating up like a sauna, the receiver wet against his ear. He switched it to the other ear.

"You have to think of the future, Brodie. Make plans, decide what you want to do, and get started. It's no good just drifting."

But that's just it, Brodie thought, *I don't* know *what I want to do.*

"But Dad says he needs me as crew," he said finally. "And I've still got a lot to learn about sailing."

"Of course you do – you didn't sail as a kid like your father. But he'll drive you crazy with his orders – do this, do that – I can hear him now."

So can I, Brodie thought. He opened the door to get some air, but a jackhammer started up in the marina's parking lot and he had to close it again.

"Let him find someone else to crew. There're lots of guys with nothing better to do than sail to the South Seas. Tell him to buy you a plane ticket back here right now."

Oh sure, Brodie thought, *and watch him go ballistic.* Besides, he didn't really want to live with his mother, not the way she was now. Sweat trickled under his T-shirt and down his chest.

"I've got to go, Mom. Dad said not to run up a big phone bill."

"He can't get away with this; I'll take him to court. You tell him to phone me."

Brodie stepped out of the booth and took in gulps of fresh air. Here he was in the middle again – as he had been ever since the divorce. Whatever he did, one of them would be mad at him. The twitch in his right eyelid started again.

Why did it matter so much to them which one he lived with? Maybe it was an ego thing, for as far as he could tell, neither of them liked him that much. It had been his older brother, Blake, they had treasured. His mother still kept Blake's picture in every room of her condo all these years later, his ashes in an urn on the mantle. Not that he didn't understand.

He was in no hurry to go back to *B* dock. What was he going to say when he got there? He walked slowly along the main dock, hands in his pockets, staring into the brown water around the marina. A fluorescent circle drifted by, giving off the pungent-sweet smell of gasoline. He watched the rainbow-colored circle expand and contract with the waves. It pulsated in and out, in and out, in and out. . . .

Brodie had sensed that his older brother was special early on, when he was just little. He could recall playing with his fire truck on the floor and hearing his parents brag to each other about Blake: how he led the class in math, how he fixed his bike himself, how resourceful he was. He'd tried hard to be like Blake, but the more he tried the less he succeeded. It was like walking in shoes that didn't fit.

He remembered his mother crying quietly for months after the accident, her beloved piano abandoned in the living room. He'd never heard her play or sing since. He remembered, too, his own sense of loss, and a confusion of other feelings.

Later, when his parents separated and his mom moved to Florida, he visited her during school breaks. When she came home from work, he'd grab something to eat and make an excuse to go out before one of her drinking buddies in the condo came over. At first he wandered the streets, until he found a library that stayed open in the evening.

Back in Ottawa, his father had changed too. He'd thrown himself into his job, working nights and weekends and getting a big promotion. When he *was* at home, they didn't talk much. Never about anything that mattered. But, in Ottawa, Brodie had friends from school to hang out with. As was his nature, whatever they suggested he went along with. That got him in trouble when they were on a hike and broke into an empty cottage. All they took was a package of cookies, but they were seen. A stern lecture by the police and their parents followed. "Stop just hanging around," his father had said, "and find something you want to do." *Easy to say.*

The move came out of the blue. His father was terminated from his civil service job in a government cutback. Bitter at losing the position he'd worked long and hard for, he sold the house and, in a grand gesture, bought an older forty-foot sloop already set up for cruising. "Get away from this frigid place forever," he'd said. Brodie went along.

The sloop happened to be berthed in Puerto Rico. They flew there before Christmas and Brodie switched to a school near the marina, while his father spent the rest of the winter readying the boat for the Pacific crossing.

He'd had to choose between staying with his father or going to live with his mother. Eventually he'd have to choose a country too. Born in the U.S. of an American mother and a Canadian father, he had dual citizenship for now. All these decisions — family, country, future — made his head ache.

It was with more than a little uneasiness that he'd decided to stay with his father. He didn't know much about sailing. It would be exciting crossing the Pacific, but what if he was seasick all the time? And what about those monster typhoons he was always reading about?

Brodie'd come to with a start as a Puerto Rican family piled onto the dock from their cruiser. He watched them stroll by. The father's arm was draped around his son's shoulders; a smaller child was clutching his other arm. They were laughing about the father's missing shoe, which had apparently been kicked overboard. Brodie followed them as far as *B* dock. There, he hesitated.

His father was on the deck of *Southern Cross*, checking the rigging. He had to decide what to tell him about the phone call. Taking a deep breath, he headed down the dock.

"Well, what did she have to say this time?" his father asked, as he climbed back on board.

Brodie watched a frigate bird torment a gull until the gull dropped the fish it was carrying. With an acrobatic swoop, the frigate bird snatched the fish out of the air before it hit the water.

His father looked up sharply. "Well?" Metal squealed against metal as he gave another twist to a turnbuckle he was tightening.

Brodie shrugged. "The usual. Nothing special."

His father's expression relaxed. "That's good," he said. "That's very good. I thought she might try to talk you out of it."

"Well, she did want me to go back and stay with her," Brodie admitted.

"I thought she was off to some meditation retreat in California."

"She is. Only for a few weeks though."

His father grimaced. "Let's hope it does her some good."

"When are we leaving?" Brodie asked.

"Saturday. We could go Friday, but starting a voyage on a Friday is supposed to be bad luck." His father tugged on a shroud to test its tension, like a cowboy checking a saddle girth before mounting. "I bought a chart of the western Caribbean today," he said. "Shows the hazards to avoid on the way to the Panama Canal – like the Colombian coast, where the drug traffickers are. Have a good look at it before we leave. And here's a list of things that still need doing before Saturday."

They'd pulled out Saturday just after dawn. Brodie wondered what it would be like. His father had been teaching him sailing since they'd moved onto the boat, but this was his first real offshore experience.

"Here we go on the voyage of a lifetime," his father said. He was jauntier than usual as he guided *Southern Cross* between the red and green buoys at the mouth of the harbor.

Watching him, Brodie remembered what he'd overheard a grizzled sailor say about two people on a long voyage. Either you grow to hate each other, or you become much closer. He wondered which it would be....

3

Brodie leapt down the companionway calling, "Dad! Dad!" He jerked open the door to the rear cabin. *Empty!* He raced forward to the V–berth at the bow. No sleeping form there.

Then he knew. "Dad! Oh, Jesus, Dad!"

He tore back up the companionway, stumbling on the steps in his haste, bloodying his shin. In the cockpit, he jumped up on the bench seat and stared behind at the wake of *Southern Cross. Nothing!*

He felt nausea well up in his stomach and buried his face in his hands at the picture that leapt to mind – his father falling overboard, calling out, watching helplessly as the boat sailed away. Then waiting, waiting for the sharks. . . .

Stop it, Brodie! Put your brain in gear. It's up to you to find him. You'll have to run the boat by yourself. First . . . first what? He tried desperately to remember the man overboard procedure. *Something important . . . before anything else.* He couldn't think. *What is it?* Then it came to him.

Get the compass reading, that's it! He jumped down from the bench and peered at the illuminated compass in front of the wheel — 240 degrees, it told him. Still the same southwesterly course held by the windvane self-steering.

Now what? . . . Now come about . . . come about and head back exactly the way we came — 180 degrees in the opposite direction. He stared at the compass, trying to work it out, his mind in turmoil, his eyelid twitching. *Hurry — every minute takes us farther away!*

Finally Brodie figured it out. He'd have to come about and head northeast on a course of 60 degrees. Disengaging the self-steering, he cranked the wheel to starboard. His heart thumped crazily against his chest. He'd never done this before without his dad standing over him.

Southern Cross had been running downwind, with the sails well out to port to catch the northeasterly trade wind. She began to turn. But he had to let go of the wheel to winch in the jib so it would blow across the deck to the other side, and the boat hesitated in the middle of the turn. The bow was caught by a swell and slammed sideways. Both sails flapped wildly, cracking like gunshots, and the boom jerked back and forth as if in spasm.

Oh, God, I'm losing control! He panicked, grabbing the closest jib sheet. *Wrong one!* He dropped it, grabbed the other, and threw it around the winch. *Not that way — clockwise, stupid! There . . . damn, where's the winch handle? . . . There it is . . . now crank.*

He cranked and the jib came in and began to fill with wind, just in time to bring the bow around to complete the turn. He jumped back to the wheel, straightened the rudder, then grabbed the main sheet to haul in the main-sail. *Southern Cross* settled in the new direction. *Got that far,* he panted, *now head up until the compass says 60 degrees.*

But that proved impossible. The wind was coming at him out of the northeast – the very direction he wanted to go. The boat stalled and he had to back off. Brodie sighed. He would have to tack back and forth across the wind. It would be a long slow process.

He set the self-steering for the first tack, then jumped up on deck and planted himself by the mast, where he could see better. Gripping a shroud for balance, he scanned the sea ahead as *Southern Cross* bucked and heaved and beat its way windward.

With time now to think, after all his frantic activity, the full force of what had happened hit him. *Dad! Overboard!* His knees buckled and he had to hold on tight to stay upright.

But if I retrace the course we took last night, I will find him. Won't I?

Southern Cross was now hammering into the very swells she had been sliding down so effortlessly a short while ago. A gust heeled the boat sharply. A huge swell lifted the bow and slammed it down again, shaking Brodie to the bone. A sheet of spray drenched him. He hung on and kept his eyes glued to the sea ahead. *Let me see you on top of the next swell, Dad. Please let me see you.*

The sky lightened; *Southern Cross* battered her way east. Suddenly it struck him. *What about the current?* He hadn't allowed for the current. *Brodie, you idiot!*

Dashing below, he collided with the drop-leaf table in the saloon when the boat pitched suddenly. A sharp pain shot through his thigh. He grabbed the chart, a ruler and pencil, and limped back to the cockpit. He didn't want even a minute to go by when he wasn't on the lookout.

He braced himself on the cockpit bench, unrolled the chart, shielding it from the wind and spray with his body, and followed his father's pencil line, marking their progress since they'd left Puerto Rico. They didn't have GPS to give them their exact position – his father had been waiting to buy one cheaply in Panama. In the meantime he'd got by, estimating their position each shift by averaging the speed from the knotmeter readings and the direction from the compass. Dead reckoning, his father called it. When Brodie first heard the term, he thought it meant you'd be dead if you reckoned wrong. *Maybe that's not far off,* he thought now.

His father's pencil line ended halfway between Puerto Rico and the Panama Canal. The Caribbean current there, Brodie noted, flows northwest at two knots. He chewed on the pencil, figuring, keeping one eye on the sea ahead. Then he lay the chart on the bench to draw a vector for the current.

A sheet of spray flew back. He snatched the chart up again – too late, it was soaked. He stared at the soggy mess for a full minute, his shoulders slumping. Without the chart, he'd be lost. He picked it up carefully, took it below, and spread it out on the bunk to dry. He'd have to guess at a correction for the current and pray he was close enough.

It was full daylight now, the sky a brilliant blue and cloudless. Still the light revealed nothing ahead but rolling swells topped by white, like dabs of whipped cream. Each time *Southern Cross* mounted one, it was only to reveal more. Swells to the horizon. Nothing else.

Dad gone! He still could hardly take it in. He pictured his face now – the creases grown deeper lately from worries, the lean frame thinner. *Where are you, Dad? I need you. Will I ever see you again?*

4

All that morning, Brodie remained on the foredeck. Wind-driven spray drenched him. Still he stayed on, searching the sea, eyes straining. Once an hour he made his way back to the cockpit to tack – one hour beating northeast of his target, one hour beating southeast. He allowed himself to dash below once to slap together a peanut butter sandwich before hurrying back up again.

He saw no sign of anything, not even another boat on the horizon. Not surprising here – most sailors stayed well away from the Colombian coast while en route to or from the Panama Canal. They were already closer to Colombia than they'd planned to be as a northerly wind had hit yesterday morning and driven them south. "Stay well offshore while passing Colombia," the cruising guides advised, "and steer clear of any suspicious craft." If he did come across another boat, would he dare contact it? He'd read about the drug running, the pirating of yachts, the kidnappings. . . .

He wished they still had the old single sideband radio for long-distance communication. But it had died and, after days of tinkering with it, his father had thrown it overboard in a fit of frustration. That left only the VHF with its short range – twenty nautical miles or so – good for calling in for directions when approaching a harbor, but little use out here. Brodie called anyway, on the emergency channel as his father had shown him, but he wasn't surprised when no one answered.

Now he glanced at his watch. Time to tack again.

Nervously, he talked himself through it. *Right, disconnect the self-steering, now spin the wheel, let go one jib sheet, winch in the other, quick now, adjust the main like Dad said . . . no, the other way . . . there, the jib's pulling well, now reset the self-steering. Done. You're getting better at it, Brodie.*

Back at his post on deck, spray stung his face and ran down his cheeks. He coughed, spitting out a mouthful of salty water. He'd heard that beating east from this corner of the Caribbean – against the wind, against the swells, against the strong current – was one of the roughest passages in the world. Sailors talked about the fearsome waves created when the sea, driven by the trade wind all the way from Africa, piled up against Central America. He understood now why so many small-boat sailors chose to sail west, rather than east, when they set out from here to make their way around the world.

How long should I keep on beating east? What if I go too far? I might sail right by Dad without spotting him. He went over it again. *Let's see, he could have gone overboard anytime between midnight and four. Say it was the middle of his shift, two o'clock. That would mean the boat sailed downwind for two and a half hours by herself before I turned her around. At eight knots, that's twenty nautical miles. But we're probably only making two knots back, what with beating and tacking and all. So it'll take a good ten hours to go back the twenty miles. That would mean between two and three this afternoon.*

Will that be too late? Is it too late already? How much longer can Dad stay afloat? How much longer can the boat take this pounding? How much longer before something breaks? How much longer can I go on?

He was bone weary. It was already time to tack again.

Making his way back to his lookout post after the tack, his foot suddenly skidded out from under him. He lurched, grabbing the lifeline to save himself. He looked down, rubbed the slippery spot on the deck, and sniffed.

Grease! Even with the salt spray soaking the deck, it was still greasy.

Suddenly he remembered — yesterday afternoon on the rollicking downwind run. *Was it only yesterday?* His father had asked him to grease a sticking block up here on the deck. He'd overdone it and a fat blob of grease had plopped onto the deck. He'd meant to come back with a rag, but was distracted by the sight of dolphins playing in the bow wave and forgot. The grease was still there, like a booby trap.

A chill went through him. *Is that what happened? Did Dad slip on the grease and lose his balance?* He pictured him tumbling over the lifeline into the sea. Because he, Brodie, had been careless. For the second time that day, he felt like he was going to throw up.

The more he thought about it, the more convinced he became — his neglect had started the whole horrendous chain of events. There had to be some reason his cautious father had gone overboard, and that was likely it.

Brodie, it's all your fault!

By the time he reached his post by the mast, he knew he wouldn't give up. No matter what it took.

Hours later. Still nothing. Hours of *Southern Cross* hammering into a swell, staggering, shaking it off, plunging into a valley, then rearing up just in time to meet the next swell.

Every mile east was a battle, but their progress, though slow, was steady. By two o'clock, Brodie began to worry about overshooting the mark. By three, he decided it was time — time to stop and begin a search pattern. *He likely went overboard around here somewhere,* he thought.

He turned the key and cranked the diesel into life, then headed into the wind and lowered the sails. He began to circle. Small circles at first, then larger. It was nerve-racking, in such wild seas. On the downhill runs he had to fight the tendency of *Southern Cross* to slew sideways. Motoring across the swells was even worse — each time the boat rolled, he held his breath until she righted again.

He circled all afternoon, until the sun began to sink. Nothing. . . .

As darkness closed in, Brodie stared into the gloom. He'd felt alone most of his life, but never this alone, never this vulnerable. Somehow he must get help. He couldn't do it by himself anymore. One searcher wasn't enough.

Go for help, right now, Brodie. Head for the nearest port as fast as you can. Why waste a whole night out here when you can't see anything anyway? By tomorrow, with luck, more boats could be out here searching with him.

Then he remembered that the nearest port was on the Colombian coast – the coast where the drug mafia ruled, where pirating and kidnapping were everyday events. *But there must be people with boats there who would help me,* he thought, *people other than the drug runners. . . .*

He went below and smoothed out the wrinkled chart, now almost dry. The scale confused him at first, until he remembered that a nautical mile is only slightly longer than a regular mile. The closest point of land lay less than a hundred nautical miles to the south. He had to piece together a rip to make out the name. GUAJIRA PENINSULA, it said. He stared at it. The northernmost point of South America, the Guajira Peninsula, jutted out into the Caribbean Sea like a fist, daring him to come closer.

Venezuela would be safer, he knew, but that would mean at least another day of beating east against the wind and the two-knot current. No time for that. He needed help right now. He steeled himself. He would head across the wind on a fast reach. To the Guajira Peninsula, Colombia or not.

5

Southern Cross made good time reaching across the wind, but the swells coming at her from the side made handling difficult. Afraid to leave it to the self-steering, Brodie stayed at the wheel, rigid with tension. He imagined every possible calamity – a wave breaking over the side, filling the cockpit; a stay parting under the strain and the mast toppling in a tangle of wires; a container, fallen off a freighter, puncturing the hull and the sea pouring in. It was going to be a long night.

He tried to divert his mind from all the possibilities by thinking about the books he'd read in the past year. One in particular, *The Horse's Mouth* by Joyce Cary, had stayed with him. The story of the eccentric artist Gulley Jimson struck home. The part that resonated the most with Brodie was when Gulley's mother told him not to hate his uncle – the uncle who'd been so hard on Gulley when he was growing up. Hate was a very bad poison, she warned him, and he mustn't let that feeling stay one minute.

Gulley heeded her warning then, and again later as a struggling artist when a smug critic belittled his paintings. He had to remind himself over and over that he must not let hate poison his life. Brodie found these words helped him when his father ranted on about something Brodie had done (or not done).

He remembered a time when he'd come close to hating his father. He'd arrived home from a softball game with a black eye. His father didn't have to say anything, Brodie could tell by the way he laughed that his father didn't believe Brodie'd been hit by the ball, that he thought he'd been the loser in a fight and was lying about it. "I don't lie," Brodie had said, storming out. *Funny how you never forget a little thing like that.*

The night crept by. His resolve faltered more than once and he was tempted to come about and run from the unknown coast ahead. But there was no alternative. He pressed on. At one o'clock he estimated his position and marked it on the chart. *Halfway,* he told himself. *Halfway to Colombia.*

Behind the wheel, he fought to keep his eyes open. "Closing in on land can be the most hazardous part of sailing," his father had said. But by two o'clock, he had to give in — had to take a chance on the self-steering handling the swells and the alarm clock waking him before he reached land. He couldn't stay awake one minute longer.

Brodie slept in the cockpit, first setting two alarm clocks and placing them beside his ear. Still he worried that he would sleep through, not wake up until *Southern*

Cross slammed into the shore. Like the sailor in one of the first round-the-world races who didn't wake up in time and whose boat ran right up on an island in midocean.

He was surprised to find himself leaping up at the first *ding* of the first alarm. He'd been in the middle of a dream – his father teaching him to swim, telling him not to worry, to trust him. *There were some good times once,* he thought. *He taught me swimming and canoeing. What changed him? Blake's death? Losing his job? The divorce? Or me?*

He shook the stiffness out of his legs. The sky was lightening and he could make out the coast in the distance – a thin ragged line, like it was drawn by a shaky hand. His long night would soon be over.

I'll put this night in my journal when I have time, he thought. Painful as it might be, he would put in everything that had happened since yesterday morning. He called it a journal because he thought "diary" sounded frivolous. There was no shortage of material. The other sailors they encountered at the marina all had stories – the Norwegian who didn't believe in engines, who'd built his own boat and sailed it around the world without one, sculling the heavy wooden craft in and out of tight harbors; the American who'd emerged with only scratches from crawling through cacti when his boat had been driven aground in a hurricane. There were tragedies too: the story of the Frenchwoman, shot dead by pirates in the China Sea when she'd brandished a gun, hoping to protect her family by scaring them off.

Now there was the search for his father to record. *But how will that story end?*

As the morning progressed, *Southern Cross* drew nearer the land and he saw what looked like sand dunes. Nothing moving. No sign of life. *The Guajira Peninsula? Hard to tell for sure. No identifying buoys, certainly no lighthouses on this desertlike shore.*

He hurried below, grabbed the atlas from the shelf, and flipped to the map of Colombia. It showed the northern tip of the Guajira Peninsula as semidesert all right. That was likely it then. So now he would sail southwest along the peninsula to the first town or village and ask for help.

6

As he closed in on the Guajira, hot sand-laden winds blew off the desert, heeling *Southern Cross* sharply. Brodie's lips, dry and cracked from sun and salt, bled as he bit into them. The sand raked his cheeks, blurred his vision.

A gust, the fiercest yet, hit suddenly, laying *Southern Cross* over on her side. The mainsail hovered just inches above the waves. Taken by surprise, Brodie lost his grip on the wheel and was slammed against the cockpit bench.

Don't go over, don't go over, he prayed, as the rail dipped under the water. Clawing his way back up to the wheel, he leaned into it with all his strength to force the bow to windward. *Come on, come on.*

For a moment it was touch and go, then the boat responded, heading into the wind and righting herself. That gave him time to shorten sail. He quickly rolled the jib in halfway. Then he jumped up on deck and lowered the mainsail partway. But the halyard slipped through his fingers and the sail slid all the way down and tumbled over his head. He had to fight his way out of the folds of Dacron and haul it back up. Remembering what his father had told him, he managed to tie in a reef — a messy one, but good enough he hoped.

Even with less sail, *Southern Cross* barreled along. They passed a wide, sheltered bay marked on the chart as BAHIA HONDA. His shoulders ached, his stomach rumbled, and he realized he hadn't eaten since yesterday. He stared at the bay, tempted to put in for a short rest and a meal. But these remote bays were said to be the hangouts of drug mafia, who would shoot an intruder as casually as a wild pig. He pressed on.

Eventually the desert gave way to scrubland, with lofty mountains in the background. The gusts eased, and finally he saw what he'd been looking for — the glint of sun on corrugated tin roofs to the south.

At that moment he caught a movement behind him, out of the corner of his eye. A rusty trawler, on the same course as *Southern Cross,* was overtaking him on the starboard side. Still half a mile away, it was coming up fast. The first vessel he'd seen in days. Maybe they would help him in his search.

He was wary, though. Drug runners had been known to take over yachts for their own use. Just dump the owners, who were never heard from again.

He watched the trawler grow in size. It was headed the wrong way for running drugs, he reasoned; maybe it was just a plain ordinary fishing boat. On the other hand, the trawler might have made a transfer at sea and could be heading back to port for the next load. He reached for his father's binoculars, swaying on a hook inside the companionway.

When he focused, Brodie was startled to find he was looking at a man, also with binoculars, who was staring back at him. And the man had a rifle slung over his shoulder. That decided him. He changed course to widen the gap between them.

The man on the deck pointed, and the trawler veered sharply and headed straight at him. His heart skipped a beat. There was no way he could outrun a trawler. He could only watch helplessly as it drew closer.

He saw a second, taller man appear on the deck beside the first. From the way they were gesturing, the two seemed to be arguing. Then the taller one climbed back to the wheelhouse and the trawler made an abrupt turn back to starboard. Once again it took up its course towards the roofs to the south.

Brodie heaved a huge sigh of relief. He spilled wind from the sails until *Southern Cross* was dawdling along, well behind the trawler. *What now?* he wondered. *Can I slip into the port behind the trawler without attracting their attention again?*

As he approached, he saw the town had only a small harbor. He motored cautiously around the point, catching a whiff of diesel fumes. The trawler was in the process of tying up at the wharf, the throaty roar of its powerful diesel belying its shabby appearance. The only other boats were small open fishing boats riding on mooring lines tied to trees. Two fishermen, barefoot, in ragged pants and wide-brimmed hats, were repairing nets on the shore.

The fishermen stopped their work and stared as Brodie motored by the harbor mouth. *Do I dare?* he wondered. He remembered the trawlermen's rifle and their interest in him. Maybe he should keep going, find another port. He stared seaward. No, there wasn't time. He'd have to take a chance. They did leave him alone in the end. *Just motor right in and get it over with.* He wheeled *Southern Cross* about.

He selected a spot as far from the trawler as he could get. Twenty-five feet, the depth finder said. That was about the right depth for anchoring, his dad had said, but would the bottom provide good holding? Only one way to tell.

Brodie shifted into neutral and hurried forward to drop the anchor. By then *Southern Cross* had drifted close to the rocks and he had to rush back to the wheel and circle again. The fishermen watching him smiled. With the anchor sitting in its chock ready to drop, he shifted again into neutral, waited until *Southern Cross* glided to a stop, then ran forward and released the anchor.

He let out a hundred feet of chain and cleated it. Back in the cockpit, he gunned the engine in reverse and waited to see what happened. The anchor held. He switched off and listened, struck by the sudden silence.

There was no sign of the men on the trawler now, no sign of anyone except the two fishermen and a lone donkey grazing on the hillside. Brodie sat back and felt some of the tension draining from him. He'd made it all the way here and he was securely anchored.

He wanted to sit for a while, savoring the moment. It was a relief to be out of the howling wind and drenching spray, to be calmly at anchor instead of tossed about. But a new challenge faced him now: getting help in this strange and, by all accounts, dangerous country.

He stood and stretched, stiff after the long night behind the wheel. Then he went below and gathered up his own passport, his father's, and forty dollars in American money that he found in his father's case. When he emerged, he slid the companionway door in place, locked it, patted the cabin top, and promised *Southern Cross* he wouldn't be long.

Launching the little dinghy, he rowed toward the sagging wharf. He hoped he would be able to convince the harbormaster to contact the authorities and get a search going today. He glided quietly up behind the trawler, shipped the oars, and started to climb out. Then he froze.

A voice was coming from the trawler, a voice raised in protest, a voice that seemed familiar. Before he could react, he heard a second voice, louder, threatening. Then a brief ruckus and three men emerged onto the dock.

Brodie stared. Two were the trawlermen he'd seen through the binoculars. The third was an older man, sandwiched between the two. Brodie couldn't see him clearly. The trawlermen appeared to have a firm hold on him — like a prisoner, he thought. Then he got a better look.

The erect posture, the thinning hair, the same striped shirt. Even from the back there was no doubt. It was him, bedraggled but alive!

It was so unexpected, he was tongue-tied. His father glanced back for a second and their eyes met. In that instant he saw his father give an almost imperceptible shake of his head before he was marched roughly along the wharf.

Brodie, about to call out, caught himself. He saw his father signaling from behind his back. They used hand signals on the boat — better than shouting against a howling wind — so Brodie knew exactly what the signal meant. It meant *Stop. Wait.*

He waited. He didn't understand why, but he waited until the three men rounded the corner of a decrepit shed at the end of the wharf. Then he couldn't stand it any longer. He climbed onto the wharf and followed.

7

Brodie's head was spinning. At first a surge of relief that his father was alive, then the disturbing sight of him being hustled along between those two rough-looking men. All he had were questions: *How did he get here? Who are those men and where are they taking him? And why didn't he want to speak to me? What's going on?*

Reaching the corner of the shed, he caught sight of the trio a block ahead. He followed, along a street lined on both sides with mean one-room hovels. *Whatever's happening now, he's still alive,* he kept telling himself. *He didn't drown.*

Waves of heat rose around him. He passed doors opening onto the street, caught glimpses of dirt floors and dark rooms. The men ahead suddenly wheeled down a side street. Brodie picked up his pace, but when he got to the corner there was no sign of them.

The short potholed street went nowhere, ending in a barren field. He stopped. *They must have gone into one of the houses. But which one?*

A group of kids, preschoolers, played in the dirt in front of one of the small houses. The only other person on the street was a boy kicking a soccer ball against a peeling stucco wall. The ball ricocheted off the wall and rolled toward Brodie. Instinctively, he soccer-kicked it back.

For a moment, the boy stared at him. Then, as if deciding this stranger was better than no one, he dribbled the ball down the street toward Brodie, skillfully manipulating it between the potholes.

As the boy reached him, Brodie stretched out a foot to block the ball, guessing he was expected to challenge. He hoped he'd guessed right. Maybe this boy would tell him where the men had gone.

Flashing a sudden grin, moving fast, the boy dribbled the ball neatly around Brodie's outstretched leg. Then he wheeled and spurted back down the street with it, as if it was attached to his foot. He watched Brodie over his shoulder, brown eyes taunting. *Come and get it.*

The boy was slight, fine-featured, with tousled dark hair. *About fifteen, same age as me,* Brodie guessed. He was fast but so was Brodie, who caught up and managed to poke the ball away before they both went down in a heap of tangled legs.

The boy sat up. "What's your name?" he asked in Spanish, "demanded" more like it. This was *his* territory.

Brodie brushed dirt from his jeans. "Brodie. What's yours?"

"Carlos," the boy said. "What are you doing here?"

Brodie stared down the street. "Looking for someone." Brown eyes bored into his. "Those three men," he said. "Did you see where they went?"

The boy got up, picked up the ball. "Maybe." He waited. The boy kept the ball in the air with his foot. "Why do you want to know?"

Brodie hesitated. How much should he reveal? Whose side was this kid on? "It's important to me," he ventured. "Where are they?"

The boy passed the ball from one foot to the other, keeping it in the air. "You ask questions but you don't answer any."

Brodie shrugged. "You don't either."

The boy let the ball drop. His eyes narrowed. "I don't know you. We have to be careful here."

It's like a cat-and-mouse game, Brodie thought. He hoped he was the cat, but he had an uneasy feeling he was the mouse.

Suddenly a commotion broke out halfway down the street. A man was trying to drag a goat from the yard of one of the houses. Bleating frantically, the goat dug in its feet, but the man had a firm hold on its rope halter and was winning the tug-of-war. An elderly woman was screaming and trying vainly to stop him.

"Grandma!" the boy yelled, and sprinted to her side. He tried to wrestle the rope from the man, but was pushed roughly away.

Brodie ran to help. The man kicked at him, but he dodged and grabbed the rope where it circled the goat's neck. With the boy helping him and the grandmother hanging on to the tail, they were able to hold the goat back. For a moment it was a stalemate, everyone pulling and yelling, the unfortunate goat in the middle being yanked in two directions.

Then, red-faced and scowling, the man dropped the rope. "I'll be back," he threatened, as he stalked off. "And if you still haven't got the money you owe me, I'll take more than your goat."

"You wouldn't dare," the boy's grandmother shouted after him. She turned to Carlos. "He knows I have friends," she said. "And he'd never get anyone else to rent this dump."

"But he'll be back, Grandma," the boy said. "We'll have to watch Enrique all the time."

His grandmother sighed. "I know." She suddenly realized that Brodie was there. "Thank you so much for helping us. You made all the difference."

"Yes, thank you, Brodie," the boy said. He pronounced it Bro*dee*. He stroked the goat's head to calm him. *"Pobre Enrique,"* he said, "that man would have taken you if there hadn't been three of us." The goat nickered softly, and the grandmother led him back to his small patch of brown grass.

After she left, the boy nodded at a house at the end of the street. "They went in there," he said.

Brodie was still thinking about the man who tried to take the goat. "Huh? Who did?"

"Those men you were following. They went into the last house — the one by the field."

The house was larger and set apart from the other houses. Brodie stared at it. His father was a captive behind those walls. So close. Yet, now that he knew, what could he do? He could hardly go up and knock at the door, or hang around outside waiting.

He saw that two scrubby trees sat in the field, close by the house. About the right distance apart for goal-posts. "Goalie or striker?" he asked, kicking the ball toward the trees.

The boy's face broke out in a wide grin. "Either," he said. So they took turns.

Brodie kept an eye on the house while they played. In the heat of the day, he soon had to strip off his sweat-soaked shirt. Over and over they alternated shooting and blocking shots, the boy deadly serious about his soccer. When he scored, he cheered and raced in circles, arm raised in triumph.

Suddenly Brodie heard voices and the front door of the house opened. A man came out, one of the two who brought his father here — the tall one. The man looked around cautiously and Brodie dropped his gaze. When he dared look again, the man was striding up the street.

"I have to go," he said, snatching up his shirt.

The boy nodded. "Where do you live?"

Brodie hesitated. *But I have to trust someone,* he decided, *I'm in a country I know nothing about.* "On a boat.

Down there," he said, gesturing in the direction of the harbor. Then he turned and hurried after the tall man.

He followed as closely as he dared, hoping his tan and his brown hair were enough for him to blend in. Most of the people he passed were Indian, or mixtures of Indian, Spanish, and African.

The man ahead turned suddenly and looked back. Brodie ducked quickly into an open door. The interior of the shanty he'd stepped into was so dark it took him a minute to realize he wasn't alone. A haggard-looking mother with a baby in her arms was staring at him in alarm, and a little boy with a swollen belly gazed up at him from the dirt floor.

"*Lo siento*," Brodie apologized, and, peering around the doorway, saw the man continuing up the street. He felt in his pocket for a coin, handed it to the child, and left.

When his quarry reached the main street, Brodie saw him veer into a bar. LA CUCARACHA, a faded sign said. The stale smell of beer wafted from the doorway and salsa played at full volume. Brodie chanced a glance inside. His man was seated at a table, talking intently to a fat older man seated opposite him. The fat man wiped the sweat from his face with a red bandana as he listened. From his expression, it was apparent he didn't like what he was hearing. When the bartender arrived with beer, they stopped talking and looked up. Brodie slipped by the doorway before they could spot him.

He found a dusty concrete bench across the road in the town square where he could sit and think. A mangy dog, ribs protruding, gazed up at him. A donkey loaded with sacks of yucca plodded past, led by a small boy.

His first instinct was to find a policeman and report his father's kidnapping — or whatever it was. But the police would want to know who he was and where he'd come from. And that, he knew, could mean trouble. For he had yet to legally enter the country.

Brodie stood up. He knew he'd better check in with Customs and Immigration before they found out he'd arrived by boat and was wandering around unannounced on Colombian soil. His father had had enough bad experiences with Caribbean customs officers for Brodie to know they acted like little kings, especially with yachties. No excuses — break their rules and you were in big trouble. They could even seize your boat.

He'd better get that over with, then find the police station. Customs and Immigration would be somewhere near the waterfront, he guessed. He crossed the square, then the road, and headed back toward the wharf.

Busy with his thoughts, he didn't notice that the boy called Carlos was shadowing him closely.

8

Robert Bailey shifted awkwardly, trying to ease the ropes cutting into his wrists and ankles. He winced. His efforts only made the pain worse. He could hear the two men arguing in the other room, as they had been on and off since they'd tied him up and shoved him in here.

Then he heard a door slam and there was silence.

He looked around for something sharp to cut his ropes. The scantily furnished room didn't offer much – a rickety table, two wooden chairs, a bare ceiling bulb, turned off at present. The one small window was shuttered. He began to wriggle his way over to it. At least it gave him something to do besides wonder what was going to happen to him.

He'd once read an article about kidnapping in Colombia. There were three thousand a year, it said, many by guerrillas, but also by narcos and paramilitaries. Colombia was the kidnapping capital of the world. A substantial ransom was, of course, what the kidnappers were after. But Robert knew there was no one left who cared enough about him to come up with a ransom. *He* knew that, but these men didn't. And they didn't believe him when he tried, in his halting Spanish, to tell them.

To them he was a *norteamericano* who had somehow fallen off his yacht and, by a stroke of good fortune, been delivered into their hands. And *norteamericanos* with yachts were always rich, they insisted. Which was a joke, Robert thought – if only they knew how many yachties lived hand-to-mouth, taking odd jobs so they could keep cruising.

The men had demanded his nationality, address, business, wife's name. When he told them he was divorced, they wanted his father's address. "The cemetery, unfortunately," he told them. At that point the smaller one had threatened him with a gun. Name of his company then, he'd demanded. *Norteamericanos* worked for companies, didn't they? Wealthy companies that would pay huge ransoms.

"There is no company," he told them. He tried to explain that his job had disappeared, that that was why he had gone sailing, but his Spanish wasn't up to it. More threats followed. Finally they tied him up and shoved him into this room. To think about it, he supposed.

Mostly he thought about Brodie, and the boat. He was worried that Brodie, impetuous Brodie, would get involved. The last thing he wanted was to put him in danger too. He'd been stunned when he saw him at the wharf. *How had he come to be there?* Then, as he thought about, it began to make sense. He could picture Brodie searching fruitlessly for him, then deciding to seek help in the nearest port. And this was the nearest port. It must have been hard going for Brodie to sail *Southern Cross* here by himself. He wouldn't have believed he could do it. Yet somehow he did.

He could only hope now that Brodie'd understood his signal and knew enough not to get mixed up in this mess. For, even if Brodie found a policeman in this out-of-the-way place, Robert doubted that would do much good. As the article said, Colombian kidnappers were seldom caught. They simply melted away into the jungle or the mountains with their captives. The kidnapping of one more wealthy Colombian or foreigner had become an everyday event.

Besides Brodie, he worried about the boat. So far these men had no way to connect *Southern Cross* with him. If they did make the connection, they would probably take the boat too, as part of the ransom.

Alternately humping and straightening, like a caterpillar, he slowly inched toward the window. Panting, dripping sweat, he'd almost reached it when the door was flung open and the light switched on.

He looked up, blinking. It was the smaller of the two men, the ferret-faced one, a cigarette dangling from the thin line of his lips. He stared at his prisoner suspiciously and bent over to check the ropes. Robert could feel the heat from his cigarette.

Satisfied, the man grunted and straightened up.

"*Agua, por favor,*" Robert said, licking his lips.

The man considered, then nodded curtly and went out, leaving the door open. In the other room, Robert could make out a sagging sofa and a table with cards and a bottle on it. Now that the light was on, he could also see there was nothing he could use under the window he had worked so hard to get to — it appeared that the floor had been recently swept clean.

The man came back with a soup can filled with water. CAMPBELL'S, the red label said. He yanked Robert's head up and held the can to his lips. Robert gulped it down. "*Gracias,*" he said. He caught only part of the man's muttered response. Something about being worth more to them alive than dead.

If only ferret-face knew, he thought. He wasn't worth much either way. Robert surveyed his captor's hard eyes. Just as well he didn't know, he decided.

The front door slammed and the second man came back. Robert watched the two as they stood talking in the other room. They seemed an unlikely pair. A foot taller and younger, the second man had the lanky gait and rugged look of a cowboy. Talking rapidly, he seemed agitated.

His partner nodded toward the open door, apparently concerned that Robert might understand what was being said. He strode over, reached in, snapped off the light, and slammed the door, leaving Robert in the dark once more.

He had, in fact, understood a bit of what the tall one said — something about the boss being angry, and then about being followed. And he'd caught the word *muchacho*.

Robert sighed. He knew who the *muchacho* must be. Brodie, no doubt. Despite his signal to him, Brodie must have followed them. And the tall man had, of course, noticed him. In a day of unlucky happenings, this was one more. First falling overboard, then being picked up by narcos, now they'd spotted Brodie. Bad things always happen in threes, he thought glumly.

He'd been sure his luck had turned when the trawler suddenly appeared, practically on top of him, as he was struggling to stay afloat. What luck that they had stumbled across him. Or so he thought, until they fished him out and locked him up in a tiny storeroom, stinking of sweat and diesel fuel.

The enormous relief at being saved from drowning turned to doubt about his fate at the hands of his rescuers. They certainly weren't ordinary fishermen, he'd realized. Who they were and what they were doing out there didn't dawn on him until many hours later when the trawler's engine throttled back and he heard the men hailing another vessel — a larger one; he could tell from the throb of its engines. Then came scurrying sounds overhead, the thump of a heavy line landing on the deck, followed by shouting and the growl of a winch from the larger boat.

A transfer at sea, he'd realized. Drugs, no doubt. But he himself was not transferred with the drugs. The two men on the trawler had kept him hidden.

Robert had no room to lie down in the windowless storeroom. Wedged in with cans of diesel fuel, buckets, mops, funnels, and old ropes, he'd crouched in a daze on a pile of oily rags. So much had happened to him that day. . . .

One misstep had started the whole disastrous chain of events. One crucial misstep in the dark, when he'd put his foot down on something slick on the foredeck – what, he didn't know – lost his balance, fell awkwardly against the lifeline, made a desperate grab for it, missed, and toppled into the sea. Then the sailor's worst nightmare: watching your boat sail away from you.

He'd shouted for Brodie, but he knew how deeply he slept. As the white stern of *Southern Cross* was swallowed up by the dark, he could only watch and blame himself for not clipping on his safety harness, could only wait and hope and try to stay afloat.

As the hours crept by, the past came back to haunt him – the tragic accident that took Blake, the breakup of his marriage, his father's lingering death, the loss of his job, the worry about Brodie's future. Now this unforeseen catastrophe. . . .

"Damn, damn, damn, damn!" he found himself shouting to the empty sea and sky. They'd looked on implacably.

Gradually he calmed down. *Forget about the past*, he told himself. *What's done is done, concentrate on staying afloat.* A swell lifted him and he looked for a ship's lights.

Then the swell broke over his head and he came up spitting salt water and rubbing his stinging eyes.

His one hope had been that Brodie would wake up soon and find he was gone. But even if he did wake up, Robert doubted he would know what to do. It tried his patience to get the boy moving. He remembered looking at the time just before he'd made the fatal trip to the foredeck to free the jib sheet, which had somehow wrapped itself around a cleat. Quarter to two, his watch had said. Brodie could even sleep till dawn with no one there to wake him. At least he was in tropical waters, not somewhere off the coast of Canada, where hypothermia would finish him in no time.

But tropical waters were home to sharks. He swiveled, looking nervously for telltale fins. How long before they sniffed him out? he'd wondered.

He alternately floated and tread water. *Save your energy,* he'd told himself, *no point in swimming — nowhere to swim to.* As the time passed, he grew more and more resigned to the hopelessness of his situation. *Just a short trip on deck,* he'd told himself. *It'd only take a minute to free the jib sheet.* He'd broken his own rule to always clip on his safety harness when on the deck at night, and he was paying for it. Paying dearly.

Dawn had brought a renewal of hope. A fat clump of sargasso weed, teeming with tiny crabs and other sea creatures, drifted by and he latched on to it to give himself a little more buoyance. He wished so hard for *Southern Cross* to appear that he began hallucinating her image on top of each swell. But she didn't come; nothing came. As the long day passed, he drifted in and out of consciousness.

And then, suddenly, as he was about to give up, rescue. Not the white hull of *Southern Cross,* but a rusty trawler coming straight at him. He heard the helmsman shout and throttle back. A startled face peered at him over the rail as the trawler pulled alongside.

Now Robert shifted to ease a cramp in his leg and listened to the voices in the other room. The trawler had delivered him from one nightmare into another.

2

Brodie had no luck finding Customs and Immigration. He couldn't even find a harbormaster. He found a busy market and was hailed by vendors offering papayas, bananas, limp lettuce, and scrawny live chickens. He found hole-in-the-wall grocery stores; he found a Catholic church — one of the few substantial buildings in town; he found another bar pumping out Colombian songs with their infectious beat, but he couldn't find anything resembling a Customs and Immigration office.

Back at the wharf, he decided to approach the two fishermen. Shyly, he greeted them and asked his question. Bent over their nets, working their needles with gnarled hands, they appeared puzzled.

"Customs? Here?" one of them said. "What for? No one uses this harbor anymore — except the narcos, when they load a shipment on the trawler."

"And no customs man wants to be around when that happens," the other laughed.

"What about a harbormaster?" asked Brodie.

"A what?" the first one said. "What's that?"

Brodie made his way back to the main street. Well then, he decided, he just wouldn't worry about being in the country illegally. He reached the square and sat down on the bench again to think. What should he do? There wasn't anyone he could ask. His mother was somewhere in California. There didn't seem to be any such thing as a phone booth here. Was there a Canadian embassy in Colombia? Probably, but where? And what could they do, anyway? No, it was up to him.

The mangy dog was still there, begging. Brodie bought a tamale and gave half of it to the dog, who gulped it down ravenously. A vendor, long strips of colorful lottery tickets around his neck, approached. *"Lotería?"*

Brodie shook his head. *"No, gracias."* He asked for directions to the police station.

"That way," the man said, pointing. "A yellow house."

Brodie got up. "Be careful, *muchacho*," the man added. "No one goes there unless they have to."

What did he mean by that? Brodie wondered. *Where else would you go if you needed help?*

A formidable stone wall topped by broken glass surrounded the yellow house. *To keep people out or keep them in?* Brodie wondered. He reached for the iron gate.

An arm thrust in front of him, holding the gate shut.

"Carlos! Where did you come from?"

"Don't go in there," he said quietly.

"Why not? I have to do *something*."

Carlos edged away, beckoning. "Come."

Reluctantly, Brodie followed him back to the square. The lottery-ticket seller was hovering nearby. Carlos sat on the bench and waited until the man moved out of earshot before he spoke. "The person you were looking for this morning – the one the two men took into the house – is he your father?"

Brodie hesitated.

"Your uncle, maybe?"

"My father," Brodie said. "How did you know?"

"I guessed."

Brodie paced in front of the bench. "Why don't you want me to go to the police?"

"They won't do anything, and they'll give you trouble."

"Why?"

Carlos rubbed his thumb and fingers together – the universal Latino gesture for payola.

But Carlos could be in league with those men, Brodie thought. *They could have sent him to steer me away from the police.* "Why are you telling me this?" he demanded. "You hardly know me."

"You helped Grandma and me," Carlos said. "So I will help you." His liquid eyes gazed at Brodie, almost pleading. "Don't go to the police."

Looking into those eyes, Brodie made his decision. He stopped pacing and sat down beside him. "Who are the men holding my father?"

Carlos's face hardened. "Narcos. I hate them."

"Why?"

"They killed my brother."

Brodie gaped. "Those guys?!"

Carlos nodded. "The little one, Pablo. It's no secret, broad daylight, everyone knows. But it was really the syndicate. They ordered him to do it. Pablo's a gangster. He'll do anything for money – running drugs, kidnapping, even killing."

"Why would the syndicate want him to kill your brother?"

"It's a long story," Carlos said. "It's the story of Colombia." He fell silent.

He's going to leave it at that, Brodie thought. *I don't blame him.*

Then Carlos started to speak again and, once he got going, the whole story spilled out of him. It seemed that his brother had, like many young men in the town, gotten involved with the drug traffickers – the one way to make money in a place where there are few legitimate jobs. Small things at first, like unloading truckloads of drugs onto boats. As they got to know him, the narcos trusted him with more important jobs, guarding shipments and intimidating rivals.

Almost before he knew it, Carlos went on, his brother became one of them. A violent business. Frequent murders, never prosecuted. But one day, a rival syndicate struck back. His brother was gunned down in the street. "Right here in the square," Carlos said. He stared at a spot near the bench. "I collected his body."

Following his gaze, Brodie saw a faded, reddish brown stain in the concrete. He shuddered. *This isn't Canada,* he thought. "I'm sorry, Carlos" was all he could think of to say.

Brodie watched a pickup circle the square, the loudspeaker on top loudly proclaiming the virtues of a candidate for mayor. "What will they do with my father?" he asked.

Carlos shrugged. "What they always do. Keep him for ransom. And they'll ask plenty for a *norteamericano* from a yacht — half a million, a million maybe."

Brodie's mouth dropped. "But there's no one to pay that kind of money. No one to pay *any* money."

Carlos stared at him in surprise. "Your father's business partners?"

Brodie explained the situation. No business partners. No business. No job at all anymore. His father was on his own, living on a pension.

"Your family, then."

"Dad's parents are dead. He's divorced and my mother has no money to speak of."

"Your boat, then? It must be worth a lot."

"Not that much," Brodie said. "She's old, and she's all we've got left. She's our home."

Carlos absorbed this for a moment. "But they won't believe there's no money. They'll hide him somewhere and wait — maybe for a long time." He gestured at the hazy peaks of the Sierra Nevada de Santa Marta in the distance. "Probably they'll make a deal with the guerrillas in the mountains to keep him for a share of the ransom."

"But those two guys are narcos, you said!"

"Sure, but narcos deal with the guerrillas all the time. They have to pay them safe-passage money anyway, when they go into the mountains to buy marijuana and coca from the farmers."

Brodie stared at the ground. "What can I do, then?" The dog sidled up to him and he reached down to pet it. It shied away a few feet, collapsed on the cement, and gazed up at him.

"There *is* one chance," Carlos said.

Brodie perked up. "What's that?"

The lottery-ticket seller wandered by again, peddling his wares. Carlos got up. "Tell you later. But if that boat is all you've got, you'd better move it. Once word gets out, it'll be fair game for all the thieves in town."

Brodie jumped up. "I'll move her, then. But where?"

"I know a place," Carlos said. "And about your father, I have an idea, but it'll take time — and nerve."

Brodie was already crossing the road. "Let's go, then. What are we waiting for?"

10

Brodie broke into a run. He pictured *Southern Cross* ransacked, stripped of sails, lines, winches, the cabin trashed.

"Slow down," Carlos called. He caught up to Brodie and grabbed his arm. "You'll only attract attention. No one runs here." But the best he could do was slow him to a brisk walk.

As they skirted the old shed, Brodie looked anxiously across the harbor. *Southern Cross* appeared intact. He jumped into the dinghy and waited for Carlos to follow. But Carlos had stopped in his tracks at his first sight of *Southern Cross*. "Beautiful," he breathed.

Brodie fit the oars into the oarlocks. "Get in," he said.

"And so big," Carlos added. "Can you really sail it all by yourself?"

"Oh, sure," Brodie said, feigning nonchalance. He had to admit he liked hearing the admiration in Carlos's voice. *Well, why not?* he told himself. *I did sail her all by myself and it wasn't easy.*

Aboard *Southern Cross,* Carlos scooted below, examining everything. In the cockpit, Brodie unrolled the chart. He could hear Carlos exclaiming over the saloon and the galley.

"I've been studying the chart," he said, when Carlos came back up. "Lots of bays. Where would the boat be safest?"

"Not around here," Carlos said. He inspected one of the shiny stainless steel winches, stroking it as if it were a fine piece of sculpture. "Besides, we have to go where we can find help to free your father." He turned to Brodie. "It's a long hard journey. You up to that?"

Brodie didn't hesitate. "Of course. Where do we have to go?"

"First that way," Carlos said, pointing along the coast to the west, "to Barranquilla."

Tracing the coastline on the chart, Brodie found Barranquilla. A big city, it looked like, at the mouth of a vast winding river called the Magdalena. The river flowed from the mountains in the interior north to the Caribbean, effectively cutting Colombia in half.

"Okay, to Barranquilla, and then where?"

"Then up the Magdalena River."

"In the boat?"

Carlos shook his head. "The Magdalena is full of silt and sandbars. Only paddle wheelers can go up the Magdalena, or *chalupas.*"

"*Chalupas?*"

"Small motor launches."

"Okay. We go up the Magdalena. Then where?"

"To a place called Barrancabermeja."

"But what do we do with *Southern Cross* if we can't take her up the river?"

"I know someone we can leave her with."

Brodie frowned.

"Don't worry. They'll take good care of her. They're my relatives — Wayúu people, same tribe as Grandma. They live on a *finca* on the coast, on the way to Barranquilla. And you can do Grandma and me a big favor at the same time."

"How?"

"Let me bring Enrique."

Brodie blanched. "You want to bring him on the boat?"

"It's the only way we can keep him away from that man," Carlos said. "And he would be better off at the *finca*."

Brodie pictured the goat rampaging around the deck, chewing sails, breaking instruments, pooping everywhere.

Carlos seemed to read his mind. "He's quite tame," he said. "And I'll clean up his messes."

"Well . . . all right, then," Brodie agreed, though he had an uneasy feeling about it.

Carlos was already climbing into the dinghy. "Good. I'll go get him right now and let Grandma know. She'll be happy."

"What about your parents? They won't mind you leaving?"

Carlos didn't answer. Brodie untied the line that secured the dinghy. Then he watched Carlos row in circles, going nowhere.

"Want me to row you in?"

Carlos shook his head. "I'll get the hang of it. I watched you." Mouth set, he persisted until, finally, he had the dinghy heading more or less in the right direction.

Brodie smiled as Carlos zigged and zagged to the dock with determination. *There's something appealing about the guy,* he thought. It wasn't till Carlos was gone that he realized he hadn't asked him why they had to go up the Magdalena River to a place called Barrancabermeja. Wasn't that a long way from the Sierra Nevada mountains?

He set about readying the boat to sail. In the middle of straightening up the galley, he suddenly realized how hungry he was. Since his father's disappearance, he'd had only quick bites. And that had been . . . when? He thought back to the night before and his rough all-night passage to Colombia, then to the previous day and the long hours of searching. So only a day and a half since he'd first found himself alone on the boat, yet it seemed so long ago.

He got out a frying pan, lit the propane stove, and scrambled three eggs. He examined the two remaining loaves of bread, cut two slices from the one that looked the less stale, toasted them over the propane burner, and finished the last of a tin of jam.

His father had planned to restock in Panama for their Pacific crossing. Now there was no point in restocking at all if he and Carlos were going to be leaving the boat behind. Besides, he had a feeling he would need what little money he had for their journey. A long hard journey, Carlos had warned him.

By the time he'd eaten, stowed everything loose in the cabin, neatly coiled the sheets and halyards scattered about the deck, and made the sails ready for hoisting, the tropical night had descended – suddenly, as it does – and the stars were popping out, one after another.

But there was no sign of Carlos.

Brodie sat in the cockpit in the dark, staring toward the wharf, hoping to catch sight of the dinghy weaving its way toward him. *What's taking him so long? Maybe he's having trouble with the goat.*

Clouds moved in from the east and gradually extinguished the stars, like a curtain being pulled across the heavens. The darkness was complete. Brodie became more and more uneasy. *Where's Carlos?* He didn't know much about the guy. *Has he skipped out, gone for good? No, Carlos isn't that kind of a guy,* he kept telling himself. But the longer he was gone, the less sure he was of that.

He was wondering what to do if he didn't come back at all, when he heard his name being called softly.

"Brodee. . . ."

Peering over the side, he saw a face looking up at him from the water. "Carlos!"

"*Shhh!* Help me up."

"Go to the stern," Brodie whispered. *Why is he whispering?* "I'll lower the ladder." When Carlos stood dripping in the cockpit, Brodie asked, "What happened to the dinghy?" His first thought was that someone had stolen it.

"The dinghy's okay," Carlos said quietly. "Come below and I'll tell you. But no lights."

Brodie dug out a towel, a shirt, and his extra pair of jeans. He held them out. "A little big for you, but they'll do for now." Carlos ducked into the head to change. Brodie thought that odd as there weren't any lights on, but shrugged it off as shyness.

"So what's this all about?" he asked, when Carlos reappeared. "Why did you have to swim over?"

Carlos was a silhouette toweling his hair. "Because they're watching us," he said.

11

"What!" said Brodie. "Who's watching us?"

"Those guys who kidnapped your father, one of them anyway, the short guy."

"The one who shot your brother?"

"That's him. Pablo. The other's a fat man with a cigar. Don something. He's the boss. It's his trawler. He's the one who pays off the police. He's rich, into everything."

The fat guy, the one I saw in the bar, Brodie thought.

"They must have come while I was at Grandma's," Carlos went on. "When I got back to the dock, I heard them. They were sitting in the back of the trawler, just sitting there talking in the dark, so I thought I'd better listen. I snuck along the dock to where I could hear. Turns out they're watching *Southern Cross*, waiting for you to show up. They don't know you're already on board."

"But what do they want?"

"They're on to you. They've figured out you're connected with the *norteamericano* they fished from the sea.

Probably plan on grabbing you as well when you show up — and the yacht."

"If they're watching, we can't leave."

"Not now. We have to wait them out. They may decide you're not coming back tonight and give up."

Brodie had a sudden thought. "What happened to the goat?"

"I left him tied up on the beach — by those fishing boats, you know. I figured it would be easier to get him in the dinghy from the beach."

They waited, talking softly in the dark. "I heard the boss say he wanted your father out of his house," Carlos said.

"That's his house?"

Carlos nodded. "One of his houses. So Pablo said they'd take your father to the mountains if the boss would make a deal with the guerrillas to hide him. The fat man said he would, but he wasn't happy about it. Said they should have stuck to their job of delivering drugs and left the thinking to him. 'The sooner you get that gringo out of my house and up in the mountains, the better,' I heard him say."

Brodie winced. He pictured his father being force-marched up rugged mountain terrain.

They sat in the cabin, waiting. Brodie found it easy to talk in the dark — as if his voice belonged to someone else. He told Carlos everything that had happened from the time he'd woken up and found his father missing. How he had to handle the boat by himself for the first time; how he'd searched and searched until dark. The only thing he left out was the blob of grease on the deck — he felt so guilty about it that he didn't think he could ever tell anyone.

"You've been through a lot," Carlos said, sympathetically. He laid his hand on Brodie's arm.

Brodie stood up quickly. "I'll just see what's happening."

"Still there," he said, when he came back down. "I can see the glow of a cigar. I hope Enrique's all right on the beach by himself."

"He's patient," Carlos said. "He's a Colombian."

"One thing puzzles me, Carlos," Brodie said. "Why are we going up the Magdalena? Isn't that a long way from the Sierra Nevada mountains?"

"A long way," Carlos agreed. "But that's where we'll find the only person who can help us."

"Who's that?"

Carlos didn't respond. Brodie waited.

"The thing is, I'm sworn to secrecy," Carlos said at last. "But I know I can trust you. It's my older brother, Rafael." He looked around furtively.

"You know there's no one here but us," Brodie said gently.

"I know," Carlos said, embarrassed. "But Rafael is with the guerrillas in the Magdalena Valley. He's a *subco-mandante*. If the paramilitaries knew that, they would come after my family — what's left of us. But when we find him, I'm sure Rafael can help us. You see, he knows the guerrillas in the Sierra Nevadas very well. That was where he started out before he was moved to the Magdalena Valley."

"But I don't understand," Brodie persisted. "Why would your brother help to free my father? He doesn't know me – I'm just another foreigner."

Carlos smiled. "No you're not, you're my friend. And any friend of mine is a friend of my family. That's the way things work in Colombia."

Brodie liked that idea. They sat in silence. He yawned; his head drooped.

Someone was shaking him. *Must be my turn on watch,* Brodie thought. As he came to, he saw it was Carlos, not his father, leaning over him.

"Looks like they've gone," Carlos said.

Brodie got up groggily. "Right. Let's get out of here, then." He stripped off his shirt. "My turn for a swim. I'll bring the dinghy back and we can go get Enrique."

Picking up the goat in the dark was not easy. Enrique didn't want anything to do with the dinghy. The goat dug in his feet and refused to budge. Carlos took a carrot from a bag he'd hidden behind a log and enticed him to the water's edge. Enrique demolished the carrot, but wouldn't go one step further.

Then Carlos pulled out a cabbage and laid it in the dinghy. Enrique approached, eyeing Brodie suspiciously. He stretched out his neck and began nibbling at the cabbage.

"You grab his front legs and I'll grab the rear ones," Carlos hissed. "Quick, while he's distracted."

But Enrique thrashed out and all three went down in a heap. Brodie was the first up. Enrique scrambled to his feet and butted him. "Hey, you said he was tame."

Carlos grabbed the halter. "He doesn't take to strangers. You stay back. I'll settle him down." He crooned softly in the goat's ear and led him back to the cabbage. Then, with Carlos coaxing and gently lifting his feet one at a time, Enrique stepped over the stern board and stood in the dinghy, calmly demolishing the cabbage.

Brodie rowed while Carlos soothed the goat. Back on *Southern Cross,* he rigged up a rope harness and lowered it to Carlos, who fitted it around Enrique. Then he lifted him with a block and tackle and swung him onto the deck, using the boom. Enrique shook himself and urinated on the cabin top.

Carlos led the goat to the stern, out of the way, while Brodie raised the main. It flapped noisily in the wind, followed by the clank of chain as he hauled up the anchor. "Hope nobody heard that," he said, when he came back to take the wheel. "I don't dare start the engine. There's just enough wind to sail out of here."

They set out, tacking back and forth, each tack taking them closer to the harbor mouth, until finally *Southern Cross* slid silently between the headlands. The red glow of the compass was the only visible light.

Once outside the harbor, the wind and waves picked up. Brodie could see Carlos tense and grab for support as

Southern Cross heeled over. "Don't worry. It's all right," he said.

Brodie steered north to gain offing from the coast before turning west. Looking back he could still see the dark shape of the trawler, just visible against the dim lights of the town. He was about to congratulate himself on escaping undetected when he heard the roar of the trawler's diesel coming to life.

12

They stared at each other in dismay. "They're coming after us!" Carlos said. "What can we do, Bro*dee?*"

Brodie winched in the jib to coax more speed from *Southern Cross.* "With their big diesel, we can't outrun them," he said. "We might be able to lose them, though." He tried to sound optimistic. Looking back, the ghostly outline of the coast had completely disappeared. *Thank God for the clouds,* he thought. The night was still dark.

"Which way do they expect you to head?" Carlos asked.

"North, probably. North to the end of the Guajira Peninsula, then east to Venezuela for help."

"Maybe if we head west then, we'll fool them."

"Maybe," Brodie said. Trouble was, the trawler would have radar. Being drug runners, they would have everything. Suddenly an idea came to him. But it would take nerve. Could he do it?

They could hear the trawler's engine complaining loudly as it was pushed at top speed. *They must be gaining,* Brodie thought. He held his course. The seas were building, crashing against the bow as if trying to force them west. He had to fight to keep the compass needle on north.

"Shouldn't we turn?" said Carlos. "They're catching up."

"Not yet," said Brodie.

The east wind was moving them along at a good clip. But not fast enough, he knew. The trawler would be closing the gap. Still he held his course.

How long did he dare to wait? He remembered a short story by Conrad about another captain who held his course long after the first mate and the crew thought he should tack away from the approaching rocks. Only, in that story, the captain was trying to sail as close to the shore as possible so the fugitive hidden in his cabin could escape.

Now, like Conrad's captain, Brodie was holding his course until the last possible moment. But for a different reason: to lead his pursuers on a false trail north.

He stared behind into the darkness. The trawler, too, must be running without navigation lights. It might appear at any moment, switch on its searchlight and they would be trapped, held in its beam like a deer in the headlights. Yet he must take the chance. He had to keep going until the men were convinced by their radar that he was headed north.

Carlos was watching him, one arm around Enrique, steadying the goat as the swells rocked the yacht. The noise of the trawler engine was louder now. "They'll be on us any minute, Bro*dee*," he warned.

Still Brodie hesitated. *Just a little longer,* he thought. The minutes ticked by.

"All right," he said. "Hang on, here we go. I'll need your help." He cranked the wheel to port, then let go. "You take the wheel," he told a startled Carlos. "Head her due west. Two hundred seventy degrees on the compass." He jumped to the winches to ease out the main and the jib. *Southern Cross* swung gracefully through 90 degrees.

"Good. Now hold her steady there, Carlos," he said over his shoulder as he set the sails for the new course downwind. Then he stepped up on the deck and hurried forward to the mast. When he came back, he was carrying a strange-looking, hexagonal contraption made of aluminum foil.

"What's that?" Carlos asked.

"The radar reflector. It belongs at the top of the mast. I left it up until we turned so they would be sure to spot us heading north." He pitched the device down the companionway. "Without it, I expect they'll have trouble picking us up again."

He looked behind. Was it his imagination, or could he still hear an engine?

The minutes passed. Suddenly it seemed quieter. *Maybe we've done it,* he thought.

He saw that Carlos was having trouble. The bow swung wildly back and forth with Carlos constantly oversteering. The swells coming up from behind on the downwind run were tricky, lifting the stern and shoving the bow downhill at an alarming rate.

Brodie showed him how to anticipate the swells and make only small corrections, and the boat settled down. Enrique stood beside Carlos, staring at the red glow from the compass as if he were checking the reading.

Brodie went forward to adjust the jib, now blanketed by the main and flapping uselessly. He hauled the sail across the deck and poled it out on the other side with the whisker pole. Immediately, *Southern Cross* picked up speed. *Sooner or later those guys will figure out we changed course,* he thought as he worked. *The farther away we can get before that happens, the better our chances are.*

He stared ahead, alert for red or green lights that would indicate another craft coming toward them. Running without lights, without even a radar reflector, on a dark night in strange waters was asking for a collision. But in Brodie's mind, it was the lesser of two evils.

A shout brought him running back to the cockpit. Carlos was twisted about, staring behind. "The dinghy!" he said, pointing anxiously. "I thought it was coming right into the cockpit. It almost flipped over. Here it comes again."

Brodie watched the dinghy gyrate violently down the slope of a swell. He held his breath until it recovered, then watched it drift back to the end of its tether before it was brought up short with a violent jerk to start the cycle again. A mistake – he should have lifted the little dinghy on board before they'd set sail. He realized he still had a lot to learn. But there was nothing he could do now except cross his fingers and hope it survived the beating.

"I'll take over, Carlos," he said. "Get something to eat and have a rest down below. I'll need you to relieve me again later."

But Carlos shook his head stubbornly. "I'll just grab something quick and come back up. Enrique will get restless if I stay below."

Sure enough, as soon as Carlos disappeared down the companionway, the goat brushed past Brodie in pursuit.

"Come back," Brodie called, but Enrique ignored him and poked his head down the companionway. The boat lurched and the goat staggered, almost falling. Brodie grabbed the halter to pull him back, but Enrique braced his feet and stayed where he was, his neck in the cavity of the companionway like some strange headless apparition. He stayed there until Carlos reappeared with a plate of food. Then he followed him docilely back to his place.

Carlos shared a sandwich and a carrot with the goat, and settled back on the cockpit bench. Soon he was asleep, head nodding.

For two hours more, Brodie stayed at the wheel, keeping a constant lookout ahead and behind. With the moon and stars obscured, a freighter could come on them suddenly. The darkness had been their ally, helping them to lose the trawler, but he knew it could be their enemy too.

He yawned, exhausted from the strain of the chase. It was good to know he didn't have to go through another night with no one to relieve him. Had they really eluded their pursuers? It seemed too easy. Still, leading them north may have done it. He was proud of his trick with the radar reflector. He stood behind the wheel, more confident of his sailing skills now. Behind him, he could hear the comforting sound of Enrique chewing.

They took turns on watch through the night, making good time on the downwind run, sometimes clocking eight to ten knots on the knotmeter. At first light, Brodie was back at the wheel. He studied the sea behind them anxiously as the darkness lifted.

It was empty. No pursuer in sight. To the south he could make out the low-lying coast they were running parallel to.

Before long the tops of office towers on the coast came into view. Their upper windows glinted in the early-morning light, shooting out dazzling reflections from the sun.

Carlos woke up and saw the towers. "That must be Santa Marta," he said. "It's halfway to Barranquilla. The *finca* is past it, over there somewhere." He pointed to the southwest, beyond the port.

"I'd better have a look at the chart," Brodie said. "Take over, will you?"

He was conscious of Carlos's eyes on him as he swung down the companionway. Brodie's moods affected the way he moved. When he was unsure of himself, he would move tentatively. But this morning, he was feeling upbeat. They had a plan and they were on the way to try to rescue his father. He grabbed the handrails and swung down the steep steps, barely touching them with his feet.

But he was gone only a few minutes when Carlos heard a curse from below and a cry of "Oh, no!" Then Brodie's face appeared in the companionway. In his hand were a few tattered scraps of paper.

"The goat ate the chart!" he cried.

13

"I can't navigate without a chart!" Brodie glared at Enrique.

Carlos took the blame. "It's my fault, Bro*dee*. I should have watched him. He loves paper. He must have got it last night when he poked his head down the companionway."

Brodie sighed. No chart and who-knows-what up ahead! Nothing his father had taught him about navigating prepared him for this. Expensive as they were, his father bought charts for every place they planned to sail to. "Better to spend the money than run on a shoal and lose your boat," he'd said to Brodie.

He slumped on the cockpit bench, his eyelid twitching, and tried to imagine feeling his way along the strange coast. He wouldn't know if there were rocks, or shoals, or reefs, or even the depth of water to expect. He wondered if he could go on at all. Maybe this was a signal. What was the point of this wild-goose chase anyway? His father was out of reach, probably somewhere in the

Sierra Nevadas, and there was no ransom money to free him. Could Carlos's brother really help, or was that a dead end too? Maybe he should go back to school in Florida, like his mother wanted him to. Wait out the kidnappers there.

But he couldn't leave the boat. *Southern Cross* was the only possession his father had left. She was his responsibility now. If he went, he would have to sail all the way back to Florida by himself. He doubted he could do that with no one to share the watches at sea.

He looked at Carlos, now standing calmly behind the wheel. He had taken to sailing. If he would come with him they could manage, he felt sure. And he would be doing Carlos a favor at the same time. *Everybody wants to go to the States, don't they?*

"How would you like to sail with me to Florida, Carlos?" he asked, on impulse.

Carlos looked at him quizzically. "You mean, if we can't find your father?"

"Yes . . . no . . . I mean. . . ." He trailed off as the image of a fat blob of grease on the deck surfaced in his mind – an image he knew would haunt him forever if he gave up now. Suddenly he realized he was kidding himself. He would press on, no matter what. Even without a chart. "Never mind," he said. "I was just wondering."

Then Carlos said something that really surprised him. "Thanks for the offer anyway, Bro*dee*. But there's something more important I have to do here. I mean, after we free your father."

Brodie was taken aback. He'd pictured Carlos with nothing better to do than kick a soccer ball around a town slum. He'd thought he would jump at the chance. "What is it that's so important?"

"Helping the people of my country. I know it sounds crazy, but that's what I have to do — there's so much trouble here. But first, I'm going to become a lawyer." He said this as if there was no doubt about it. "I've never told anyone before."

Brodie tried not to look skeptical. "A lawyer! But law school costs a lot, doesn't it?"

"Yes, but I'll make it through somehow. I don't know how, but I will. It's all I've ever wanted to do. . . ."

"But. . . ." Brodie still couldn't quite believe that Carlos would really turn down a chance to sail to America. "All right, suppose you do find the money for law school. Then what? Who can you help, even as a lawyer?"

Carlos gave the wheel a slight turn to stay on course. "There are plenty who need help — that association of peasant women for one. They're fighting for their rights, but the paramilitaries are trying to scare them off." His eyes flared angrily. "They killed the leader's daughter, and they've kidnapped her son. People like her need all the help they can get."

Brodie could tell by his tone that Carlos meant every word. He admired him for setting a goal like that — perhaps "envied" was a better word. *A goal, any goal, that's more than I've ever had,* he thought.

Hearing Carlos's plans suddenly made him aware that, deep down, he too had a yearning to do something worthwhile. *But what?* That was the trouble, he just didn't know. Never had figured that out.

"Bro*dee?* Are you all right?"

"Huh?" He realized he was still slumped on the cockpit bench. "Oh, sure. Just thinking."

"What will we do without the chart?"

He stood up. He could do it. The old-time sailors did it all the time, didn't they? Colombus didn't have charts, neither did Magellan or Cook. No engines, either. Yet they didn't turn back. "We'll manage," he said. "You can be lookout when we get closer to shore."

"Two ships up ahead," Carlos warned.

The ships had come into view while they were talking. Freighters, heavily loaded, decks almost awash, they were already within a few miles.

Brodie studied their paths, trying to estimate if either was on a collision course with *Southern Cross*. The larger one would pass well in front of them, he decided.

Carlos pointed to it. "Looks like it's heading into Santa Marta. Must have legal cargo."

"What other kind is there?"

"Contraband. Ships with contraband go on to the Guajira Peninsula and unload secretly at night. That's how the narcos launder their drug money — buying stuff with American dollars in Panama and smuggling it in for sale in Bogotá. Some say more contraband ships come to

Colombia than legal ones. That smaller freighter may be one of them."

It was apparent now that the smaller freighter was not following the other into Santa Marta. It was continuing east, and it would pass close to *Southern Cross*. Too close for comfort, Brodie decided. "We have to alter course," he said. "Might as well head for shore and start looking for that *finca*. I'll take the wheel now."

"The *finca*'s past Santa Marta," said Carlos. "So all we have to do is sail along the shore until we spot it."

"You make it sound easy," said Brodie. "But *how* do we spot it?" He was beginning to wonder if Carlos knew just where this place was. "Have you been there?"

"Once," Carlos said. "Grandma and I went by bus, when I was little. I don't remember much, except how my aunt and uncles fussed over me."

Oh great, Brodie thought, *you don't remember much.* He waited to hear more, but Carlos had picked up the mop and was busy swabbing goat pee from the cockpit. He sang as he worked – something sad, about a lost love.

"I do remember one thing," Carlos said. He leaned over the side to rinse the mop. "A bay lined with mangroves – a huge tangle of them. The other kids liked to wade through the roots, but I was afraid to." He laughed. "I thought they would reach out and grab me, like those spooky trees in fairy tales."

"That's a start," Brodie said. "What else do you remember?"

"A round wooden house, with a thatched roof — a Wayúu house."

"I remember seeing those," said Brodie, "along the Guajira Peninsula."

Carlos thought for a moment. "And I remember one other thing — long dresses hanging on a line, bright colors. The Wayúu women make them. They should be easy to spot."

What a way to navigate a ship, Brodie thought. *Looking for brightly colored dresses on a clothesline.* "We'll have to sail in close to spot them," he said. Not only would he have to worry about unseen hazards, but also about a lee shore. "Never get trapped near a lee shore," he remembered his father warning. "With the wind against you, if your engine fails you're as good as on the rocks."

Brodie studied the wind indicator at the top of the mast. Still easterly. Should be all right as long as it didn't swing to the north. And as long as there weren't any underwater hazards.

He took a deep breath and headed *Southern Cross* toward the shore.

Now comes the crunch — closing in on the shore without a chart. He turned and glared at the goat. Enrique didn't seem perturbed.

14

Brodie sent Carlos to the bow. "Watch for waves breaking offshore. Even small breakers can mean rocks near the surface. And look for any change in water color."

"What sort of change?"

Brodie gestured at the sea around them. "From deep blue like this to light blue." Turquoise, he wanted to say, but he didn't know the word in Spanish. "Means it's getting shallow."

Carlos went forward — after giving Enrique enough carrots to keep him occupied — and stood at the bow, holding on to the forward stay for balance. They were still half a mile from shore when he called out, "Color's changing up ahead."

"Already?" Brodie called back. "What color is it?"

"Muddy."

Muddy? Then Brodie remembered. The chart had shown that the delta of the Magdalena spread over a large area. So that could be the muddy waters of the

Magdalena meeting the ocean up ahead, making it even more difficult to see underwater hazards. He peered at the depth gauge. At least he still had that. Eighty feet, it said.

Now Carlos was calling to him again, pointing behind. Brodie turned. He was surprised to see that the smaller freighter had changed course and appeared to be following them toward shore.

Carlos came back to the cockpit. "There's a man on the bridge with binoculars. He's looking this way."

"Maybe it's Colombian customs," said Brodie. The freighter was still a quarter mile away.

"No," said Carlos. "It's flying a Panamanian flag. Likely they're narcos with contraband."

"But why would they be interested in us?" Brodie wondered.

"Could be they're part of the same syndicate as the trawler guys," Carlos said. "They may have radioed the freighter to keep a lookout for us."

"Whatever they're up to, they won't be able to follow us in here," Brodie said. The depth gauge, he saw, now read only thirty feet.

"Looks like they're stopping," Carlos said, "but the binoculars are still on us."

The freighter sat offshore while they continued in. Brodie waited until the depth gauge showed twenty feet, then turned into the wind, dropped the sails, and started the engine. "We'll follow the shoreline," he said.

"Have to feel our way in. The water's even murkier here."

They crept along, Brodie nervously keeping a close eye on the depth, ready to reverse at the first hint of danger. Carlos was at the bow again, staring ahead. The coast, which had been rocky, gradually changed to marshland. *A good sign,* Brodie thought, *less chance of encountering coral or rocks.* Here and there were small *fincas* with chickens and goats, and huts with fishing nets hung out to dry.

Southern Cross motored by a bay lined with mangroves. Carlos shook his head. In the distance, the freighter was still visible, drifting low in the water, like a crocodile waiting to pounce.

They rounded a headland and the first thing Brodie saw was a line of dresses — yellow, purple, green, red — flapping, as if they were waving to them.

"That's it!" Carlos cried.

Brodie turned into the bay. Then he thought again about the freighter and the binoculars following them. He couldn't take a chance on giving away *Southern Cross*'s hiding place. Reluctantly he circled, left the bay, and kept going west.

Carlos understood immediately. "Let them think we're going on to Barranquilla," he said.

It was hard to keep going in the wrong direction. The freighter slowly shrank in the distance and, finally, they saw it resume its journey east. They cheered and high-fived and Brodie wheeled *Southern Cross* around, back to what they now called the bay of flapping dresses.

He nosed the yacht in slowly, worried about shallow water. But he was able to get in quite close to the mangroves, close enough to row in with a mooring line and tie up to a tangle of sturdy roots. Then he rowed out a stern anchor so that *Southern Cross* was secured fore and aft. Nice and snug.

They had to go through the tricky business of loading Enrique into the dinghy, using the block and tackle arrangement. This time they had lots of encouragement and suggestions from the shore, for the people from the house had rushed down to greet them. From the shouted conversation, Brodie gathered that they had been expected. "The Wayúu telegraph is better than the telephone," Carlos said.

As Brodie rowed them in, Carlos was looking worried. "I hope you won't be mad at me, Bro*dee*," he said.

"Why should I be mad at you?" Brodie said, puzzled. But before Carlos had time to answer, the dinghy scraped ashore on the pebbled beach and eager hands helped them coax Enrique out.

Carlos stepped ashore and was embraced by an older woman, regal in a long purple-and-yellow dress. "How you have grown, Carlota!" the woman exclaimed. "But you've cut off your lovely long hair."

15

Carlota! She's been deceiving me all this time! "Why," he wanted to demand, "for God's sake, why?" But he couldn't; she was engulfed by her aunt and uncles.

When she was finally able to break off, she smiled wryly at him. "Forgive me," she mouthed. Then she introduced him to her great-aunt, Graciela, and Graciela's two brothers, Luis and Manuel, and he saw that he would have to wait to confront her.

Brodie was reeling at the revelation. He'd had some surprises in his life before – some good, like the time he saw the shiny red-and-black sleigh under the Christmas tree; some bad, like the time his mother sat him down and told him she was leaving. But this was the biggest surprise of all. He felt alternately foolish, deceived, and dumb. He groaned inwardly. How could he not have noticed?

It was apparent that Great-aunt Graciela was the one in charge. She told the uncles to take care of the goat and shepherded Brodie and Carlota to the house. "You must be hungry," she said. "You're both so thin, we need to feed you up."

The house was small and round, the roof thatched. Inside, they were given the seats of honor at opposite ends of the table, and platters of fried chicken, grilled fish, and yams were brought from the oven. Brodie couldn't think of anything else except Carlos suddenly becoming Carlota.

The conversation flowed so fast that he had trouble keeping up with the rapid-fire coastal Spanish. Carlota mentioned Brodie's concern about *Southern Cross* while they were away on their journey up the Magdalena. Great-aunt, for that was how Carlota addressed her, assured him they would guard the boat well, and Luis enthusiastically described how he and Manuel would camouflage it with branches.

After the meal, everyone settled outside in chairs under a huge mango tree. Chickens scratched about them. An iguana crawled slowly along a branch above Brodie's head. Great-aunt stared into the distance. "It's different here," she said. "When Carlota came before, there were other young people. Now they've all left — gone to the city to make new lives."

"Do they ever come back, Great-aunt?"

"Sometimes — on special feast days. But the old Wayúu ways are dying." She shrugged. "Can hardly expect the women to wear mantas like this to work."

She lifted her flowing robe and let it fall. "Or the men to wear *guayucas* in the office," she added, laughing.

Carlota broke up at that. "The *guayuca*," she explained to Brodie, "is a sort of loincloth. Barely covers the important parts — doesn't meet in the back."

"Those were good times when the young people were here," Great-aunt said.

"I remember a boy called Alfredo," Carlota said. "He was older than me."

"Ah, yes, Alfredo." Great-aunt sighed. "He came to see me often, but he doesn't come anymore. Didn't he teach you how to swim?"

"Yes, he did," Carlota said. "But who was he?"

"Just someone I miss very much," Great-aunt said, and Brodie noticed she changed the subject abruptly. Leaning forward, she briskly tapped Carlota on the knee. "It's time to get down to business, dear. You must tell me more about this plan of yours to help Bro*dee* and his father."

Good for you, Great-aunt, he thought. *Now, I'll find out more too.*

Carlota stayed silent for a moment, collecting her thoughts. "Well, you know that Rafael is with the guerrillas," she began. "Somewhere in the Magdalena Valley. Near Barrancabermeja."

Great-aunt nodded. "A good boy, Rafael."

"We're going to find him," Carlota went on. "And when we do, I'm sure he will be able to help Bro*dee*."

"But how?" Great-aunt shrugged, her arms spread, palms up, showing she was perplexed. "You said Bro*dee*'s father would be taken into the Sierra Nevada mountains."

"Yes," Carlota answered, without hesitation, "but Rafael knows the guerrilla leaders there. You remember, that was where he first joined them as a teenager. When your José was there."

"I remember well," Great-aunt said. She turned to Brodie. "My husband, José, God rest his soul, fought for land reform. That was why we had to leave the Guajira – our family was put on the paramilitaries' list of guerrilla supporters, the death list they call it. We were warned in time and fled." She stared around at the small plot of land and the nearby road. "Sometimes I think we should have gone farther." A shadow passed over her face. "The paramilitaries have long memories."

"Rafael is *muy simpático*," she went on, using that useful Spanish phrase that wraps up agreeable, pleasant, and kind all in one. "I know he would help you if he could, but would he dare go back to the Guajira? He'd have to pass through paramilitary checkpoints on the way. It would be very risky for him."

Brodie decided he really liked Great-aunt. For one thing, she asked all the tough questions.

"No, Bro*dee* and I will do the traveling," Carlota said. "We'll ask Rafael to write a message to his guerrilla friends, but we will deliver it."

Great-aunt looked startled. "But for you two, the trip would be very risky also. If the paramilitaries become suspicious. . . . Bro*dee* speaks Spanish well, but he does not speak like a Colombian. Forgive me, Bro*dee*."

"But you're right," Brodie said. He watched a chicken boldly scratching in the dirt between the goat's stamping feet. "My Spanish is more Puerto Rican than Colombian."

"I'll do the talking if we run into the paramilitaries," Carlota said. "To them, we'll be just two more penniless Colombian kids looking for work. Which, for me, isn't far from the truth," she added, with a grin.

"May God be with you both," Great-aunt said, stroking Carlota's cheek.

Carlota heard Enrique butting the door of the shed and went to settle him down. Great-aunt watched her as she walked away. "I am glad to see Carlota looking well," she said to Brodie. "She has gone through a lot – her father and mother murdered. . . ."

"Murdered!" Brodie exclaimed.

Great-aunt touched his arm. "Of course, you didn't know. I shouldn't have blurted it out like that."

"I'm glad you told me," Brodie said. "What happened?"

"Her father was a school teacher in guerrilla territory. He supported the farmers' fight to get better prices for their crops, and her mother ran a workshop for indigenous women's rights. One night the paramilitaries attacked and took over the town. It was a massacre." She shuddered. "Carlota's mother and father were among the victims."

"How awful."

"It was a terrible time for all of us, but especially for the children. Carlota's younger brother didn't speak for months afterward. Carlota was the strong one, but sometimes I wonder if she's keeping it all bottled up inside."

He remembered Carlota's silence when he'd asked about her parents. "And then her brother was shot by a narco killer," he said.

"Yes, and then that," Great-aunt sighed. "Will it never end?"

Once again Brodie was reminded of the story of Gulley the painter, who'd known that hate will poison your life. *Hate is poisoning a lot of lives in Colombia,* he thought.

That night, Carlota slept in her great-aunt's house. Brodie, who had to close up the boat in the morning, said he would sleep on board.

He rowed back to *Southern Cross* under a blanket of stars. Giving a final pull on the oars, he coasted and stared up at the Gemini Twins, Pollux and Castor. He remembered reading in his star guide that Castor, which appears as one star to the naked eye, is in reality a double star when looked at through a telescope.

Which reminded him, he still hadn't had a chance to talk to Carlota about her posing as a boy. Tomorrow for sure, he vowed.

Venus, the brightest object in the night sky, glittered in the west. Brodie gazed dreamily at it. Then the dinghy nudged against the side of *Southern Cross* and he climbed aboard and fell into his bunk. That night he had a weird dream.

He was in the gallery of the House of Commons back in Ottawa. When he looked down at the Speaker's chair, he saw that the Speaker was Great-aunt in a flowing robe. Carlota had the floor and was making an impassioned speech about human rights. She looked up at him. He shrank back in his seat as he realized that all he had on was a loincloth. It didn't even meet in the back. Beside him, his father, in a business suit, pretended he didn't know him.

16

The next day, Brodie battened everything down and closed up the boat. *Southern Cross* swung forlornly, like a tethered horse left behind, watching him as he rowed to shore.

The bus wasn't due until the afternoon. Great-aunt walked up the path to the road with them. They were early, not wanting to miss the one bus of the day to Barranquilla.

Great-aunt continued to probe Carlota's plan, searching for any flaw that might endanger them. "Last night I woke up," she said, "and asked myself why the guerrillas would agree to release Brodie's father. If you could pay them something that would be different, but without ransom money. . . ." She sighed. "It's not like it used to be. The guerrillas were there to help the peasants – that's why my José was such a supporter. Now it's all about kidnapping and controlling the drug-growing land, so they can make money to fight their wars. Sometimes I think they're as bad as the narcos, or the paramilitaries."

"No, the paramilitaries are the worst," Carlota said bitterly.

Great-aunt realized her mistake. "Yes, Carlota, of course you're right; they are the worst."

A cloud of dust arose in the distance. The bus was still half a mile away, but Great-aunt was suddenly in a hurry to leave. "You can flag it down," she said. "I'll go back now." She embraced Carlota and kissed Brodie's cheek, then turned and strode down the path toward the house.

As the bus drew up, Brodie saw a passenger wipe the dust from his window and stare after Great-aunt. His dark glasses glinted in the afternoon sun.

They climbed the steps and the driver swung the door shut. Brodie staggered and grabbed a post as the bus took off. "How much for two to Barranquilla?" Carlota asked.

"Eleven thousand pesos," the driver shouted, over the noise of the engine. She paid with the pesos Great-aunt had loaned them for their expenses until Brodie could change his American money. He had tried to give her dollars in exchange for the pesos, but she'd refused. "You can pay me back in pesos when you return," she'd said, and smiled. "That way you'll have to come back safely."

Brodie and Carlota made their way down the aisle, looking for two seats together. The bus lurched and Brodie had to grab the overhead rail to avoid tumbling into a stout woman's lap. *Worse than* Southern Cross *in a high sea,* he thought.

They had to settle for aisle seats across from each other. Brodie noticed that the man with the dark glasses — the one who had stared through the window at Great-aunt — watched them intently all the way to their seats. *But I'm being paranoid,* he told himself, *everyone on the bus is watching us — there's nothing else to do, that's all.* Still, as he sat down, he could feel the man's eyes burning into the back of his neck.

The air coming in the windows felt like a blast from a hot air register. He sat there sweating, his clothes sticking to his body. He glanced over at Carlota. The young man in the window seat beside her was talking animatedly. Brodie felt a twinge of jealousy. *But that's ridiculous,* he told himself. *She's only a friend and, besides, that man thinks she's a boy. Doesn't he?*

Brodie studied her — the hair shorter and darker than his, the long eyelashes framing deep brown eyes, the loose-fitting shirt and jeans that masked her real shape, the solemn expression broken every now and then by a quick smile. . . .

At a crossroad the bus jolted to a stop and a number of passengers got off. One of them, Brodie was pleased to see, was the young man next to Carlota. She shifted over and he slid in beside her.

"He's going south," she said, indicating her former seatmate. "That's the highway over there. We could go that way and eventually get to Barrancabermeja, but it would mean two long bus rides and take too much of your money. I'm hoping we can work our way there on a boat."

"All right, Carlota," he said. It felt strange now calling her that.

She frowned. "I'm still Carlos when we're in public. Please remember. It's important."

Now he was really confused. "But why?"

"I feel safer that way," she said.

"Is that really why you call yourself Carlos? I thought you were playing a trick on me."

She turned, touching his arm to reassure him. "I wouldn't do that to you, Bro*dee,* though you *were* the first one I tried it out on. When you came along, I was making plans to go on a trip on my own and I wanted to see if I could pass as a boy. I'm sorry for misleading you."

Hearing that, Brodie felt better. "Where were you planning to go?"

"To Cartagena, where the tourists are. Some friends of mine work there as street musicians. I was going to join them as a singer and try to make some money."

"You have a nice voice. I'm sorry I interfered with your plan."

"That's all right. This way I'll help you, and I'll see my brother. I'll find out more about *La Violencia* too, and what I can do when the time comes."

"Is it bad there?"

"The Magdalena Valley is the worst in the country for violence, they say. We'll have to be extra careful."

He wondered if it was wise to go there at all. Probably not. But there was no other way to seek his father's release – he should consider himself lucky he had Carlota to guide him. He leaned forward to unstick his shirt from the back of his seat and took a quick glance to the rear. The man in the dark glasses appeared to be asleep, his head flopping up and down like the Madonna-figure on springs stuck to the dash in front of the driver.

The bus started up again. They gazed out the window at the changing scenery. An immense lagoon appeared, spreading out south of the highway – vast stretches of marshland, the water tan-colored from mangrove leaves. Flocks of ducks rose, complaining at the bus's approach.

"*La Ciénaga Grande de Santa Marta,*" Carlota said.

He watched a heron take off, great wings flapping as it struggled to gain altitude. The *cienaga* went on and on – a rich world of marshland and waterbirds, seemingly peaceful. But what was underneath the peaceful surface? he wondered. Fish, no doubt, in uncounted numbers, and turtles and iguanas, but also fierce caimans and poisonous snakes.

It was almost an hour later before the *cienaga* petered out. In the distance they saw the Magdalena River itself, and soon the bus crossed a long bridge over the river and entered the outskirts of Barranquilla. Factories, markets, a sports stadium, and streets jammed with traffic were Brodie's first impressions. He felt the small bundle of dollars in his pocket and wondered where they would sleep. If they found a cheap hotel, he could pay for a night or two. *Then what?* And when they got to that dangerous place with the funny name – Barrancabermeja – where would they go at night? It was all new to him. The twitch in his eyelid started up again.

17

The *hospedaje* was the first one they came to after leaving the bus station. The paint was peeling and the sign over the door hung at an angle. An old man was snoring in a stuffed chair – the only chair in the tiny lobby – and the thin balding clerk was leaning on the counter, reading a newspaper. The clerk glanced at them suspiciously, as though they might steal the only portable item in the lobby – an ugly green ashtray overflowing with butts on a polished wooden stand. It took some talking by Carlota to convince him they were seriously interested in a room and had the money to pay.

The room was small, with two narrow beds and a bathroom down the hall in which the water dribbled from rusty taps and most of the shower tiles were missing. But the price was only twenty-five thousand pesos, which Carlota negotiated down to twenty thousand after a rapid exchange with the clerk. Twenty thousand pesos sounded like a lot to Brodie, but he felt better when he figured out it was only seven of his U.S. dollars.

They shut the door and sat down on the sagging beds. Brodie realized it was the first time they had been alone since he had learned she was a girl. He felt suddenly shy.

Carlota, however, seemed the same as before. She was all business. "We can only afford to stay one night here, Bro*dee*," she said. "We can't be wasting your money on *hospedajes*."

He stared out the grimy window at the litter in the alleyway. The sun had already disappeared behind the building across the way.

"We'll try the docks in the morning," Carlota went on. "I've heard that the boats sometimes need extra hands."

"Why don't we see what we can find out here first," Brodie suggested.

The clerk at the desk had gone back to his paper. He was staring morosely at a picture of a soccer goalie flying through the air in a vain attempt to block the ball. He merely pointed, without raising his head, when Carlota asked him where the docks were.

The old man in the lobby, who was now awake, peered at them around the wing of his chair. "Maybe I can help," he said gently. "What boat are you looking for?" He had a gravelly voice to go with his grizzled beard, watery eyes, and lined face. He was, Brodie saw as they walked over to him, a barrel-chested bear of a man.

Carlota explained that they weren't looking for a particular boat, but to find work on any boat so they could travel upriver.

He surveyed her slight build then glanced at Brodie, not much bigger. "It's tough work, you know. Hauling thick ropes, shifting barrels and crates."

"I may not be big, but I'm a hard worker," Carlota said resolutely.

"I am too," said Brodie. He wondered if they could wrestle loaded barrels.

"And we'd work for nothing," said Carlota. "In return for our passage."

"The docks are a rough place," said the old man. "And the men who work on the boats are jealous of their jobs. They won't be pleased if you two show up and say you'll work for nothing. I know, I used to be a captain myself. . . . Before I retired," he added.

Brodie heard the clerk give a snort at this. "Drank yourself out of a job, you mean," he muttered. The old man ignored the clerk's remark. *Maybe he's hard-of-hearing,* Brodie thought, for he looked like he could easily pick the clerk up with one hand if he wanted to.

Seeing Carlota's crestfallen expression, the old man spoke up again. "I do happen to know a captain who's in need of a cook temporarily. His wife, Rosa, walked out in a huff last week when he complained about her *sancocho* . . . said there wasn't enough chicken in it." He chuckled. "Rosa's left him before – always comes back after he's begged long enough – but in the meantime, he's too cheap to hire a real cook. Either of you boys cook?"

"I can make *sancocho,*" Carlota said quickly.

The old man laughed, bringing on a coughing spell. "Good for you," he rasped. "He might take you on, then. And your friend could wash dishes. Here. . . ." He patted his pockets until he found a crumpled pack of *Pielroja* cigarettes and the stub of a pencil. Tearing off a scrap of paper, he scribbled a note in a shaky hand and handed it to Carlota. "Give that to Captain Alvarez. His boat is called *La Rosa*. She's an old paddle wheeler. Good luck, now." And he sank back in his chair and resumed his nap.

"Thank you very much, Captain," Carlota and Brodie said in unison as they headed back to their room.

The clerk, as they passed, was still staring at the picture of the soccer ball eluding the Colombian goal-keeper, as though he could change the outcome if he stared at it long enough.

"You sure you can cook?" Captain Alvarez asked Carlota. "Most boys your age can't boil an egg. Spoiled rotten by their mothers, they are."

"I live with my grandmother," Carlota said, "and I do the cooking when her arthritis is acting up. *Sancocho's* her favorite."

Captain Alvarez's eyes lit up. "It is? Tell you what. Cook supper tonight, then I'll decide." He studied the note again. "How is old Alberto, anyway? He taught me all I know about the Magdalena," he said, without giving them a chance to answer. "He was the best captain on the river. Knew every sandbar. They shift, you know, but

Alberto could read the river. He could tell where the next one was going to appear. Other boats would get stuck, be there for days . . . have to unload their barges to float them off." He poured a shot of *Ron Medellín* into a glass. "But Alberto would detour around a new sandbar before anyone else even knew it was there."

The captain shook his head sadly. "The booze got to him though. One day he fell asleep at the wheel and ran full speed into a *chalupa* coming up the river. Hell of a mess. Court of inquiry. Lost his license." He eyed them over his glass. "You boys are young, just getting started, so let me give you a bit of advice: beware the demon rum." He poured himself another shot. When he saw them watching, he added, "I never drink when I'm working."

Captain Alvarez had been talking nonstop since Brodie and Carlota had come aboard. *He not only misses his wife's cooking,* Brodie thought, *he misses having her to talk to.*

It was the morning after the old man had told them about Captain Alvarez needing a cook. Finding *La Rosa* had been easy enough. Most of the other boats were motor launches, the newer *chalupas*. Beside them *La Rosa,* with her lofty wooden superstructure and her paddle wheel, looked as out of place as a Victorian matron at a disco.

Captain Alvarez saw Brodie admiring the mahogany woodwork in the cabin. "She's a fine old boat," he said. "Built way back when paddle wheelers were the queens of the Magdalena. My father was captain then." His eyes took on a dreamy look. "Lit up at night, the passengers strolling the deck, it was the only way to travel. Then the airplane came along – Colombia was the first country in South America to have an airline. From then on, the paddle wheelers went into decline." He downed the rum in his glass. "The few that are left are used only to push barges up and down the river."

A wiry man with dirt-smeared hands poked his head in the door. "Barge nearly loaded, Captain," he said. "Ready to go first thing in the morning." He looked curiously at Carlota and Brodie.

"These boys may be cooking for us on this trip, Jorge," the captain explained.

Jorge frowned.

"Captain Alberto recommended them," the captain said. "Show them the galley."

Jorge muttered darkly to himself as he led Carlota and Brodie to the galley amidships.

"Have you really made *sancocho* before? Whatever that is," Brodie asked, when Jorge had left, still muttering.

"No." Carlota selected a large pot from the lineup on the galley wall above the old wood-burning stove. "But I've watched Grandma make it many times. First you'll have to kill and pluck the chickens."

"Me!" Brodie blanched.

18

"You've never killed a chicken before?" Carlota asked, incredulously.

"I've never killed *anything*," Brodie said. "Except the occasional fish I caught — and I hated doing that."

"Well, there's a first time for everything," Carlota said. "Like me learning to row your dinghy. . . ."

"Nobody here buys a dead chicken," she continued, as they walked down the gangplank. "In this heat you want to know it's fresh."

The open-air market was noisy with the raised voices of buyers and vendors haggling over prices. Brodie wrinkled his nose at the rank smell of meat that had been sitting in the heat. He sidestepped as a man hosed down the concrete floor in front of his fruit stand, and he tried not to look at the flies circling a pile of overripe bananas.

Ahead of him, Carlota stopped at a stall to negotiate with the woman behind it. By the time Brodie got there, the woman was disappearing behind a curtain, clutching three skinny, squawking chickens. She came out a minute later with three limp birds, to Brodie's relief, and handed them over.

Carlota grinned at him. "You got lucky this time." At other stalls she bought yams, yucca, *plátanos,* peppers, onions, and garlic. "We'll get the money back from Captain Alvarez later," she said.

In the galley, Brodie chopped vegetables while Carlota plucked and cleaned the chickens. He tried not to watch too closely as she pulled out the intestines. Then, the sweat pouring from him, he stoked up the old wood-burning stove.

Jorge stuck his head in the door. His frown lessened when he saw the big pile of chicken parts and vegetables ready for the pot. "Captain'll want to eat at his usual time, boys," he warned. "Six o'clock sharp."

"No problem," Carlota said. She dumped the ingredients into the pot. "Sure hope it's ready on time," she murmured.

By the dinner hour, the aroma of chicken seasoned with onions, peppers, and garlic filled the galley. Brodie sniffed appreciatively, confident now that Carlota's dish would pass the captain's test.

He was right. After dinner, Captain Alvarez belched contentedly and told Jorge to show the boys their sleeping quarters.

"Congratulations. You got us the job," Brodie whispered, as they followed Jorge below to the dark stuffy cabin where the deckhands slept. But when they got there, he stared with dismay at the crammed-together bunks, the head with its troughlike urinal. At least there was one cubicle with a door, but still. . . .

"You can't sleep here with the deckhands, Carlota," he said. "I'll tell the captain the truth – you need a separate cabin."

"No, Bro*dee*," she said. "I've slept in worse places. Don't give me away, or everybody in the Magdalena Valley will know I'm a girl by tomorrow."

But Brodie was uneasy and he slept only in fits and starts. When the three deckhands rolled in after a night at a waterfront bar, the air was filled with macho remarks and rude noises. He looked over at Carlota but, worn-out from cooking in the hothouse of a galley, she slept through it all.

It seemed no time before Jorge was calling them to get up and begin breakfast. It was still dark.

The galley had cooled off during the night, but it heated up again when Brodie fired up the stove. Carlota fried eggs and made mounds of toast, and Brodie brewed an immense pot of strong Colombian coffee.

"Where's the *bistec?*" Jorge complained, when Brodie put the plate in front of him.

Brodie could only look puzzled.

"*Mañana,*" Carlota said quickly.

"*Bistec?*" Brodie asked her later. "For breakfast?"

"Colombian men love steak with their eggs," Carlota said. "I should have remembered. Eggs on horseback, it's called."

At six, with long blasts of her steam whistle, *La Rosa* announced she was leaving. The deckhands cast off the bow lines and Captain Alvarez let the current swing the bow out. Then he ordered the stern lines let go and *La Rosa* headed upriver, pushing the loaded barge ahead of her like a nursemaid with a pram. The big paddle wheel on the stern groaned and complained as it struggled against the swift-flowing current.

Brodie finished scrubbing the remnants of egg from the cast-iron frying pan and stepped out of the galley to watch the fast-flowing river. It was one thing, he found, to stare down at the water rushing past at a dizzying pace, another to watch the bank sliding slowly by, like a slow-motion movie. He felt that now they were really embarked on the mission to free his father, and for the first time he was hopeful.

As the morning wore on, the factories of the city outskirts gave way to dense tropical jungle, interrupted occasionally by clearings for villages and fields, like a dark green quilt with a patch of a different color here and there. *Chalupas,* loaded with passengers going downriver, hurtled by like rocket ships. Dugout canoes driven by outboards slipped along the bank.

As *La Rosa* chugged farther and farther inland, the heat intensified. Whenever Brodie had a spare minute, he leaned on the rail, catching whatever slight breeze their forward motion generated and watching the broad muddy river — swift-flowing, but meandering too, curling into bays and inlets, exploring everything in its path like a curious child before moving on. He found the Magdalena hypnotic. As he stared at it, Brodie thought about his father in the mountains and wished there was some way he, too, could know that there was hope.

Gradually the punishing sun sank lower, leaving behind the heat absorbed by the hull and the decks as a reminder that it would soon be back. When *La Rosa* stopped at a village to unload drums of kerosene, Carlota bought huge *bagres* fresh from the river for dinner. Brodie cleaned them and she fried them with onions.

That night in the steaming cabin, the deckhands flopped onto their bunks naked. Carlota fled outside and Brodie asked the captain if they could sleep on the deck "because of the heat." He shrugged. "Sleep where you like, if you can stand the mosquitoes." So they dragged their mattresses onto the lower deck for the night.

As they were serving breakfast the next morning, Captain Alvarez warned they would pass a paramilitary checkpoint that day. "They'll want to know where you're going and why," he said to Brodie, who was refilling the captain's coffee mug.

"We're going to Barrancabermeja," Brodie said.

The captain's face clouded. "That's a dangerous place these days. I thought you would come all the way with us. Why do you want to get off there?"

Brodie hesitated. Carlota had told him that Barranca-bermeja was where they would find Rafael and the guerrillas, but he certainly didn't intend to reveal that. The only other thing she'd mentioned was that it was an oil refining center.

The captain stared at him impatiently.

"We want to look for work," he blurted out.

"Work? But why there?"

Brodie searched his mind desperately for a reason. Looking up, he was relieved to see that Carlota had appeared in the doorway and was listening.

She came in with a second serving of eggs on horseback for Jorge. "Yes, any kind of work," she added. "Cooking, gardening –"

"It would be safer for you to stay with us to the end of the line," the captain interrupted. The end of the line, Brodie had learned, was La Dorada, where the river narrowed and cargoes were transferred to trucks for transport over the mountains to Bogotá. "If the paramilitaries know you want to get off at Barrancabermeja, they won't let you pass. You might be planning to join the guerrillas."

"Yes, you must stay with us all the way," Jorge agreed, as he mopped up the last of his breakfast. He leaned back and patted his stomach.

"That's settled then," the captain said. "I'll tell them you're coming with us to La Dorada."

Brodie grimaced. The first hitch in their plan.

19

"Guess we'll have to sneak off at Barranca-bermeja," Brodie said, when they got back to the galley. "I don't like doing it, though. The captain's been good to us."

The more he thought about it, the less he liked it. He was reminded of the British sloop berthed beside them at the marina in Puerto Rico – *Midnight Flit* it was named. "What's a midnight flit?" he'd asked his father.

"In England, if someone sneaks out of their room in the night without paying, they call it a midnight flit," he'd said. Brodie wondered how his father knew.

Now, however, midnight flit or not, they had no choice.

"I hate to leave the captain without a cook, too," Carlota said. "But if that's the worst we have to do on this trip, I guess we're lucky. If we want to find Rafael, we have to get off."

That afternoon two men in camouflage outfits carrying AK-47's came alongside in a small boat. Brodie, peering from the galley, was reminded of the reports of modern-day pirates seizing cargo boats. Captain Alvarez, however, slowed *La Rosa* so the men could board, and Brodie realized they must be the paramilitaries.

The men talked briefly to the captain, then prowled through the ship. Brodie heard their footsteps approach the galley. "I'll do the talking," Carlota reminded him. He busied himself peeling vegetables.

The footsteps stopped at the doorway. "Well, well, it's the two young cooks," a raspy voice said.

"What's for dinner, boys?" a second voice added scornfully.

Brodie kept peeling. Out of the corner of his eye, he saw Carlota look up from her work. "Fish," she said shortly.

"Not sure I'd want to eat it," one of them said, laughing. Suddenly his voice became harsher. "How far you two kids going?"

"All the way upriver," Carlota replied.

"Then where?" the man persisted.

"Then we'll hitch a ride to Bogotá in a truck," Carlota invented.

"What's the matter with your friend — cat got his tongue?"

Brodie looked up, his right eyelid twitching.

"Yes, you," the man said.

"I'm going with —" For an awful moment he almost said "her," but stopped himself in time and nodded at Carlota instead.

"Then make sure you keep going," the man said. "And don't come back. The last thing we need here is more young punks getting off to join the guerrillas." He turned to his companion. *"Vamanos, Ramón,"* he said, and they stomped off.

"Sure hope we never run into those two again," Brodie said.

On the third day, *La Rosa* steamed toward the high red banks from which the city of Barrancabermeja got its name. "Iron in the soil," Jorge explained.

To the south, beyond the city, the elegant steel towers of the refinery poked into the sky. A flare burned at the end of a pipe several hundred feet high, like an enormous candle stuck in the earth.

La Rosa tied up at the wharf and workmen began unloading supplies for the refinery: stacks of pipe, huge pumps and valves – their bright colors showing through the slats of crates marked MADE IN U.S.A. – two shiny new Ford pickups, cases of Russian vodka and Scotch whisky. The unloading went on until a blast from the refinery whistle stopped work for the day.

The next morning, after serving breakfast, Carlota wrote a note for the captain on a piece of cardboard torn from a cereal box.

"I thanked him for his kindness," she said. "Told him I'd left *sancocho* for tonight's dinner, and that we're very sorry but we have an urgent matter to attend to in Barranca." She looked at Brodie. "How's that sound?"

"You have the makings of a good lawyer," he said. "Just one thing more – tell him not to blame Captain Alberto." Brodie pictured the old man snoozing in his lobby chair. "Tell him Captain Alberto thought we were going all the way upriver when he recommended us."

Carlota added that, then put the note near the big pot of *sancocho* simmering on the stove, where either the captain or Jorge would be sure to find it.

They told the captain they were going to the market. "In that case, get me some mangoes," he said. "Barranca mangoes are really juicy." He smacked his lips in anticipation. That made them feel even worse about deserting and, in the end, they snuck back aboard while the captain was having his siesta and put a bag of mangoes in the galley.

"They'll be your present," Carlota said. "Paid for with your money."

"No, they're our present," Brodie said, "and it's our money," and they walked quickly away.

We've made it all the way to the Magdalena Valley, he thought, *and we're one step closer to guerrilla territory and to Rafael. Just so long as those paramilitary guys don't spot us. If they do. . . .* But he wasn't going to even think of that.

Brodie realized now what a risk Carlota was taking for him.

20

"What's going on?" Brodie said, out of the side of his mouth. For whatever street they took, it was the same: soldiers on every corner, submachine guns slung over their shoulders.

Carlota shrugged. "*Quién sabe?* But I don't like it."

In the next block they encountered more soldiers, lounging against a building, smoking. The soldiers eyed them suspiciously as they passed.

Ahead, Brodie saw what appeared to be an army barracks, with sentries on duty. He stopped and looked at Carlota. She nodded and they wheeled around the next corner, heading away as fast as they could. But now they didn't know where they were.

They were hesitant to ask directions. Carlota had thought they would find out about guerrilla activities just by keeping their eyes and ears open, but they hadn't expected to see soldiers everywhere.

Now more and more people were streaming past them from the other direction, many carrying plastic bags with yams or mangoes or bread sticking out the top. "Must be coming from the market," Carlota said. "Let's find our way there and start all over."

From the market, they set out again — in the opposite direction this time. They hadn't gone far before they suddenly realized there wasn't a soldier in sight. Still someone alert on every street corner, though. On one corner a boy stood smoking; on the next, a woman chatted to a friend. Like the soldiers, they eyed Brodie and Carlota as they passed.

"I feel like we're on TV," Brodie said. The houses, he noticed, were much shabbier in this part of the city — more shanties than houses, many cobbled together from scraps of plywood, tar paper, and old tin signs, some with the words *Cerveza,* or *Cigarillos,* or other bits of ads still showing.

They kept going. Another corner, another two boys. One of them flicked his butt away as they passed, then pulled out a pack and lit another cigarette.

"Everyone chain-smokes around here," Brodie said. "Don't they know it can kill you?"

Carlota shrugged. "Same where I live. It's crazy. They say that a bullet is going to get them before the cigarettes."

In the next block, a group of boys and girls were gathered, talking and laughing with a priest. Carlota and Brodie veered onto the road to pass. As they did, the priest turned and, lifting his hassock up out of the dust, fell in beside them.

"Good morning," he said, smiling.

They returned his greeting. He looked at them curiously. "You're new in town. . . ."

"Yes, Father," Carlota said. "We just arrived, worked our way here on a boat."

They walked another half a block before the priest broke the silence. "I don't mean to pry," he said, "but as you're new here, maybe I can be of some help."

Do we dare ask him about the guerrillas? Brodie wondered. *Better go slow.* "There is one thing that puzzles us," he said. "Before, all we saw were soldiers. Yet here, there are none."

"Where were you before?"

"We went straight into the city from the docks," Carlota said.

The priest laughed. "Ah, I see. You were lucky, boys. It's a wonder they didn't stop and question you. You walked right into the part of the city that's under army control."

"We had no idea!" Carlota exclaimed. "Then who's in control of this part?"

The priest stopped at the gate of a brick house that had seen better days. A parched lawn struggled to show a bit of green. "It's a long story," he said. He opened the gate. "If you'd like to come in, I'll tell you. You should know for your own safety.

"By the way, I'm Father César," the priest said, as he poured three tiny cups of Colombian coffee, black as ink, from a pot on the stove.

"I'm Carlos," Carlota said. Father César looked at her with a humorous expression. *Does he know?* Brodie wondered. "I'm Brodie." he said.

"Bro*dee?* An unusual name. Is it Spanish or . . . ?"

"Irish," Brodie said, then quickly added, "Colombian Irish."

"Ah." Father César took a sip of his coffee and regarded them. He put down his cup. "Let me explain about this place that puzzles you."

Barrancabermeja, he told them, was a hotbed of political unrest. The workers at the government–owned refinery felt underpaid and ill–treated. The unions tried to improve things, but had little power. So most workers supported the guerrillas, who fought for real change.

Brodie pricked up his ears at the word "guerrillas." He looked at Carlota.

"The government keeps a strong army presence in Barranca," the priest went on, "to protect their refinery. They control that part of the city, but they seldom dare to come into the barrio, where just about everyone is a guerrilla supporter."

He paused to offer coffee again. Brodie shook his head – he liked it, but was already twitchy from caffeine overload.

"Bear with me," Father César said. He smiled. "Call it what you may – priestly intuition, perhaps – but I have a feeling all this may be important to you. The guerrillas harass the army, which is helpless against their jungle tactics. So the army looks the other way when the big landowners organize paramilitary units to fight the guerrillas. The guerrillas are no angels, but the paramilitaries. . . ." Father César shuddered. "Whole families have been slaughtered because they were suspected of helping the guerrillas."

Brodie glanced at Carlota. To anyone who didn't know her well, she appeared to be listening impassively. Only the hurt in her eyes revealed her emotions.

The priest regarded them across the kitchen table. "As you may have guessed, those people you saw on street corners here are guerrilla lookouts. This city is a war zone. As a priest I'm not supposed to take sides, but I have my sympathies. Too many of my parishioners have been killed by paramilitaries."

Brodie could see Carlota's mind working. For his part, he felt they could trust Father César. But what about Carlota?

Apparently, she agreed. "My brother is with the guerrillas," she said.

"Here?"

"Somewhere near here. He's a *subcomandante*. His name is Rafael."

The priest thought for a moment. "I don't know of him, but I was posted to Barranca just six months ago — from a sheltered Bogotá seminary. Believe me, it was a shock. One killing after another." He fell silent and stared at a picture of Jesus on the wall, as if asking Him how He could let these things happen.

"It's important we find Rafael," Carlota said. "Life and death."

Father César came out of his reverie with a start. "Rafael, you say? I could ask around. But people would be more willing to tell me if they knew who wants him and why. One has to be very careful here, you understand," he added. "I need to know the whole story."

Carlota looked at Brodie. He nodded.

"Then we'll tell you, Father," Carlota said. She sighed. "But first you have to know that I'm not Rafael's brother Carlos. I'm his sister, Carlota."

Father César smiled. "I understand — a wise precaution. I'll tell only those I have to. Now go on with your story. . . ."

21

The dugout canoe slid between the banks of the stream, under a canopy of branches. It slowed to avoid a partially sunken log, then sped up again. The four occupants sat in tandem — the driver in the stern, then Carlota, Brodie, and the guide, Juan, who had brought them here.

A pair of macaws squawked at the intruders and took flight in a flash of scarlet. A caiman splashed onto the bank and waddled away. Brodie stared into the crystal-clear water and wondered about piranhas. Running his hand over the rough interior of the canoe, he felt the marks of the tools that had been used to shape it. *Must have been real craftsmen,* he thought, *who chose, felled, and hollowed out a tree this size.* It was long enough for half a dozen people, or a cargo of supplies, or the contents of many fishnets, and straight enough to hold a true course through the water.

"Almost there," Juan said, over his shoulder. The canoe rounded a bend and the driver cut the outboard and

coasted in to the bank. To Brodie it looked no different
from the overgrown banks that had been flashing by for
the past hour. Then the bushes parted and a boy with a
submachine gun stepped forward. He nodded at Juan,
unsmiling. *He's even younger than I am,* Brodie thought.

Juan and the driver jumped out and quickly slashed
off branches with their machetes to cover the canoe. Then
Juan motioned to them and they set off along a narrow
trail through the jungle. Not a word had been said.

In the lead, Juan hacked at the foliage, which reached
across the trail as if the jungle was determined to reclaim
its territory. Underfoot, the forest debris rustled as unseen
creatures scuttled away. The damp humid smell of rotting
logs and musty leaves hung in the air. Howler monkeys
marked their progress with warning calls. Mosquitoes
attacked in swarms. Brodie swatted at them futilely. Juan,
he noticed, ignored them.

Suddenly he felt a vicious sting on his ankle. He
stopped and brushed frantically at a line of red ants on
his shoe. Beside him, something heavy dropped from a
tree with a thud. He saw only the tip of its tail as the big
snake slithered away. *A boa constrictor?* He hurried to
catch up to the others.

They were challenged by a sentry and allowed to
pass, and then the trail opened up into a clearing. Around
the edge, hammocks were slung between trees. Several
tents, a table, and camp chairs sat in the center, and a
group of men and women dressed in fatigues were clus-
tered around a map on the table. They wore two-way

radios on their belts. One of the men turned and saw them.

Carlota rushed to greet him. "Rafael!"

"Carlota!" Rafael said. He hugged her. "I couldn't believe it when I got the message from Juan that you were in Barranca looking for me."

A chunky, bearded man bending over the map straightened up. His black eyes scanned them like searchlights. "We need to talk," he said to Rafael. "Over here." He nodded toward the largest tent. "The three of you." He strode to the tent and, without waiting for them, lifted the flap and disappeared inside.

"That's *Comandante* Fabio," Rafael said. "Come." While they were walking to the tent with Rafael, Carlota introduced Brodie.

The tent smelled of citronella from a smoldering mosquito coil. Brodie and Carlota shifted awkwardly under the fixed gaze of the *comandante*. "There's something you two must tell me," he said.

What can we possibly tell you? Brodie wondered.

"The army has been looking for our unit for months," the *comandante* said. "A whole battalion of them, stumbling around the countryside. Getting nowhere," he added scornfully. "Yet the two of you walk off that old paddle wheeler, *La. . . .*" He searched for the name.

"*La Rosa*," Carlota supplied.

"*La Rosa.* You've never been in Barranca before; you wander around the city like lost sheep — almost bumbling into the army barracks, I'm told — yet by the end of the first day, you have somehow found out where we are." His voice rose, "And you've even managed to send a message to your brother at this highly secret location the whole army has been searching for." He paused.

The comandante must know everything that goes on in Barranca, Brodie thought. *How does he do it?* Then he remembered the radios, and the people they saw on every street corner — the guerrilla lookouts.

The *comandante* began to pace. His voice rose again, as if it had a mind of its own. "What I want to know is this: how in God's name did you find out so quickly where your brother was?" He threw up his hands and appealed to the heavens, in this case the roof of the tent.

"Well, it was like this, *Comandante,*" Carlota said meekly. "We happened to meet Father César in the barrio —"

"Father César," the *comandante* interrupted. "The new priest?"

"Yes, but please don't blame him. I told him I had to find my brother Rafael, who was with the guerrillas, but Father César refused to say anything until we told him who we were and why we needed to find him."

"And what did you tell him?"

"That we needed Rafael's help urgently to —"

"And then?" the *comandante* broke in impatiently. "What did Father César do then?"

"He disappeared for a while, and when he came back he had Juan with him. Juan listened to our story, and said he would bring us here the next day — but only if Rafael said it was all right. I guess you know the rest."

The *comandante* stroked his beard. "You're sure no one else knew why you were in Barranca?" He fixed her with his relentless stare. "No one followed you?"

"Positive."

"And just why was it so urgent that you risk your neck — and ours — to come here and see your brother?"

"It's all because of me, *Comandante,*" Brodie said. "You see, my father was kidnapped, and Carlota said Rafael could help me because he knows the guerrillas who are holding him."

The *comandante* turned to Rafael. "Is this true?"

"If Carlota says so, I'm sure it is true," Rafael said. "But I know nothing about it until I talk to her. Who is holding Bro*dee*'s father, Carlota, and where?"

Before she could answer, a man stuck his head in the tent. "A paramilitary raid in the Barranca barrio, *Comandante,*" he said. "Message just in."

"I'm coming," the *comandante* said. He turned to go. "Work this out with your sister, Rafael, and do what you can." At the entrance, he stopped and looked back at them. "I'm glad you two aren't in the army." For the first time, the hint of a smile crossed his face. "If you were, they would have been on us long ago." He lifted the tent flap. "Oh, and one more thing, Bro*dee*. Colombian guerrillas do not 'kidnap.' They 'retain' people — people who have more than their share of wealth. When they pay a suitable tax to help the poor, they are released." He ducked out of the tent and dropped the flap.

"You'd better start at the beginning," Rafael said.

Carlota told him about her chance meeting with Brodie, her decision to help him, and how she'd happened to overhear the two men on the trawler talking about where to take Brodie's father. When she described the men, Rafael looked up sharply.

"I know those two well," he said. "The older one with the potbelly is Don Antonio — a power-hungry man."

Carlota nodded. "That's him. And the other is that thug Pablo."

"The killer," Rafael muttered.

"What about the third man — the tall one?" Brodie asked. "Looks like a cowboy."

"That's Don Antonio's son, Alfredo," Rafael said. "I went to school with him. Not a bad guy, just does what his father tells him. He and Pablo run the trawler for his father."

Carlota went on to tell about the trawler chasing them. "Now they are after the yacht, too," she said. "But Bro*dee* eluded them in the night and we sailed on to Great-aunt Graciela's *finca*. I thought it would be the best place to hide the boat while we came here."

Rafael's eyes widened. "Great-aunt Graciela's! Did you know that she and Don Antonio used to be good friends? Much more than friends, in fact."

Carlota gasped.

"He was just plain Antonio then," Rafael said. "The ambitious son of a poor farmer. He was in love with Great-aunt Graciela — she was a beauty in her day. They say he was brokenhearted when she married José instead of him."

"Great-aunt and that man. It's hard to imagine," Carlota said. "Then maybe *she* can convince him to free Bro*dee*'s father!"

Rafael shook his head. "No. They aren't friends anymore. More like enemies."

"Now I *am* confused," Carlota said.

Me too, thought Brodie.

Rafael sighed. "Years ago, the story is that Antonio and Great-aunt Graciela were . . . well, they were lovers." He stopped, flustered. "I shouldn't be telling my little sister this. . . ."

"*Dios mío,* I'm not little anymore, Rafael," Carlota said. "Go on."

"It was after her husband, José, died. Antonio was married then, but. . . ." Rafael paused. "Well, you know how it is. I guess Great-aunt was lonely, and Antonio was an old boyfriend who lived nearby. Then two things happened – nobody connected them at the time, though there were rumors. First, Great-aunt went away for a while, and then Antonio and his wife adopted a baby boy. His son Alfredo."

"Alfredo!" Carlota exclaimed. "Then is Great-aunt Alfredo's mother? Is that why he used to visit her?" She and Brodie stared at each other.

"But she said he doesn't come to see her anymore," Brodie pointed out.

"He probably doesn't dare," Rafael said. "There's

more to the story. Many years after the adoption, Antonio's wife took a bus to visit her sister. The bus went off the road in the mountains and everyone perished. After the funeral, Don Antonio went straight to Great-aunt Graciela and asked her to marry him. But she had heard too many stories about him by then."

"What kind of stories?"

"How Don Antonio made his money in drugs, and used it to buy up farmland cheap, squeezing poor farmers until they had to sell out. When he asked Great-aunt Graciela to marry him, she turned him down, told him to get out. He was furious. He never forgave her. But enough of Don Antonio. Hopefully you'll never see him again." Rafael looked at his watch. "I have to go on patrol soon. What is it I can do to help you?"

Carlota explained her plan. Rafael looked skeptical. "Certainly I'll write a letter for you. But it's a hard trek up those mountains for a couple of fourteen-year-olds."

"Fifteen," Carlota said, indignantly.

"Sorry, I lose track. I would come with you, but I can't leave here. I'm sorry, Bro*dee,* that I can't do more."

"I understand," Brodie said. "But you are doing a lot. Carlota and I will get there with your message somehow."

Rafael looked at him steadily. "Yes, I believe you will. I'll write to my friend Diego – he's the *comandante* in the Sierra Nevadas – and I will let him know your father is an old family friend." He smiled. "A bit of an exaggeration, perhaps, but I can see that you and Carlota are good friends and that makes you family. Besides, as you assure me there is no ransom money, they're wasting their time anyway. I will tell him that, too. Now come to my tent while I write the letter."

Rafael wrote on an orange crate, which served as his table. When he finished, he handed them a folded sheet of paper. "This is the letter," he said. "I hope it will do the job. I know that Diego will find a way to give your father his freedom if it is at all possible. And this," he handed them a second sheet, "is a rough map showing how to get to the guerrillas' camp. It's not easy to find your way in the Sierra Nevadas. Study the map carefully because you must burn it after you've memorized it."

"Burn it!" Brodie said.

Rafael nodded. "It would be disastrous if the wrong people got hold of it. And hide the letter well, too. Now you'd better get going. Juan is waiting to take you back."

He went with them to the edge of the clearing, then he hugged Carlota and, to Brodie's surprise, hugged him too. "Be very careful in Barranca," he said. "The place is alive with army and paramilitaries."

22

Juan led them back to the parish house. No one answered their knock, but the door was unlocked. "You can wait for Father César inside," Juan said. "He won't mind." They went in expecting Juan to follow, but when they turned to thank him he had slipped away.

Half an hour later Father César came back. He looked pale and was muttering to himself. He stopped when he saw them. "Ah, you got back safely. I'm glad. I was worried."

"Are you all right, Father?" Carlota asked.

The priest sighed. "A terrible day. Paramilitaries raided the barrio this morning. Took everyone by surprise. They did a house to house search, beat up anyone who resisted. They threatened to kill Mario Fajardo, one of the union leaders, when he tried to stop them. Fortunately a guerrilla unit arrived and drove them out."

"Who were they searching for?" Brodie asked.

"Two boys they suspect came here to join the guerrillas." Father César looked at them levelly.

Brodie's eyelid twitched.

"The word is," the priest went on, "they're street kids who got by the paramilitary checkpoint on the river and then disappeared when they reached Barranca."

"Us!" Carlota exclaimed.

"It looks like it," Father César said.

"Then we're putting your life in danger by being here, Father," Brodie said.

"You should leave for your own sakes, not mine," the priest said. "If they find you. . . ."

A knock at the door startled them. They all jumped up. "Quick! In here." Father César opened a closet door and lifted a pile of laundry off the floor. Brodie and Carlota squeezed in and crouched down, and he dumped the laundry on top of them.

The door shut and they were left in pitch blackness. Brodie pushed a shirt out of his face to get air. He couldn't hear anything except the thumping of his heart. It seemed so loud, he thought it would give them away.

Then footsteps and the closet door opened. They stayed perfectly still. But it was Father César's voice that floated in. "It's all right," he said. "It's a friend of mine."

When they emerged from the closet, Father César said, "Peter's a Mennonite from Canada. A human rights worker. Knows everything that goes on in Barranca. And this is Bro*dee* and Carlota, Peter," the priest continued. "They just arrived."

Peter held out his hand. He was looking at them curiously. *If he knows everything that goes on here,* Brodie thought, *he's probably connected us with the two kids the paramilitaries are looking for.* He took the proffered hand, which grasped his in a viselike grip.

The Mennonite was a broad-shouldered young man whose skin shone.

Carlota stared hard at him. "How can a Canadian protect our people's rights?" she demanded.

Peter replied calmly. "Just our being here helps, believe me."

"But how?" Carlota persisted.

"By making the army leery," Peter said. "They get the latest military hardware from the Americans – for free – and they want to keep getting it."

"I know," Carlota said. "To fight the drug war, they claim."

"Exactly. And the last thing the army wants is bad publicity over human rights abuses – certain American senators might cut off their military aid. So they try to rein in the paramilitaries when they know there are observers around."

"Are there many of you?" Carlota asked. Her tone had softened.

"Not enough," Peter said. "And now the Colombian government is threatening to cancel our visas. We're trying to recruit more Colombians. But, for them, it's dangerous work."

"Dangerous for you, too," Father César remarked.

Peter shrugged. "At times. How long are you staying?" he asked Brodie.

"We're leaving as soon as we can find a way back to the coast," Brodie said.

"We're hoping to work our way on a boat," Carlota added.

"I was down at the docks today," Peter said, "and I heard *La Rosa* is returning from upriver ahead of schedule."

"She is? When?"

"Tomorrow morning. She'll load drums from the refinery and then leave for Barranquilla."

Carlota and Brodie looked at each other. Did they dare?

It wasn't until Peter left that Brodie realized he hadn't just happened to drop in. He had come purposely to let them know about *La Rosa*'s return so they could get away safely.

"You can sleep in the parish hall tonight, if you wish," Father César suggested.

They waited till dark before going out. Father César unlocked the door and they slipped into the empty, darkened hall. "You should be safe," he said. "No one will know you're here. If you leave early in the morning for the docks, you'll blend in with the workers heading for the refinery."

They spread blankets on the floor to sleep on.

"I'll leave you then," the priest said.

"We can't thank you enough, Father," Carlota said.

"Yes, without you we wouldn't have known where to turn," Brodie added.

"May God keep you safe," Father César said. He peeked nervously out the door to see if the street was empty. Then he hurried away.

Early the next morning, Brodie and Carlota stepped quietly out of the hall and joined the throng of workers heading for the refinery. No one paid them any attention.

Suddenly there was a sharp report up ahead. *A car backfiring?* Brodie wondered. The crowd of pedestrians stopped in its tracks, one man in the very act of taking a step, one foot poised in the air like a statue. For a moment no one moved. Then a second report galvanized a rush for cover. Carlota grabbed Brodie's hand and pulled him into an alleyway.

"Wonder who it is this time?" a man said.

They waited. People began drifting cautiously back into the street, slowly at first, then in a rush toward the spot the shots had come from. Brodie and Carlota followed. In the next block a crowd had gathered. As they approached, they saw the crowd part to let Father César through. The priest knelt beside a body sprawled on the road.

"Too late for that," a woman near them remarked.

"Who is it?" Carlota asked.

"Mario Fajardo," she said. "The paramilitaries finished the job they started yesterday."

They stood awkwardly at the edge of the crowd, watching Father César trying to comfort a distraught young woman, her face collapsed in grief.

"Let's go," Carlota said grimly.

23

"You!" Captain Alvarez stared angrily at the two standing humbly in front of him. "You've got a nerve coming back after deserting the ship."

"We're sorry," Carlota said. "And I did leave a whole pot of *sancocho* for you, Captain," she added hopefully.

"It's my fault," Brodie put in. *Keep talking,* he told himself, *he hasn't thrown us off yet.* "There was someone I needed to see here. It was very important."

It didn't seem to be working. "Never mind the excuses." The captain waved his arms. "I've heard them all before."

Jorge appeared at the door. He took in the scene in front of him.

"Well, what do you want?" Captain Alvarez roared.

Jorge hesitated, looking back and forth from the angry captain to Brodie and Carlota.

"Well, don't just stand there, man. What is it?"

"It's uh . . . it's the deckhands, Captain."

"What about the deckhands?"

"They won't work . . . not until you get a cook. Against the rules, they say. They didn't seem to like what I cooked up for dinner last night."

The captain made a face as he remembered the awful meal. He drummed his fingers on his desk. "In the old days, they wouldn't have dared. . . ." He turned to Carlota and Brodie. "Well, what are you waiting for? Go back to the galley and get to work."

As they brushed past Jorge in the doorway, Brodie thought he saw him wink.

With *La Rosa* swept along by the current, the trip down-river was much faster than the trip up. After serving dinner that night, they were cleaning the galley when the captain strolled in. That in itself was unusual – normally he kept well clear.

"The paramilitaries were looking for you," he said levelly.

Brodie nearly dropped a plate.

"They came aboard in Barranca and did a crew count," the captain went on. "I told them you two had gone to the market and were coming back. They didn't believe me. They were right."

He picked a chicken leg out of the icebox and bit off a chunk. "You'd better make yourselves scarce when we pass the checkpoint tomorrow. Just thought I'd let you know." He strolled out chewing on the leg, then stopped in the doorway. "I'll tell them I picked up another cook and helper. You'll have to hope they don't recognize you – if they're like me, all you street kids look the same."

Carlota and Brodie looked at each other. "Maybe we should find a hiding place," Brodie said.

Carlota shook her head. "They'll search if we're not in the galley."

"Guess you're right – we'll just have to brazen it out. Maybe they'll be different men."

All the next morning they were jumpy as cats. Every time he heard a motor, Brodie looked out to see if it was the paramilitaries. Finally the dreaded moment arrived: a small boat pulled up alongside with two men in camouflage outfits. Brodie glanced out the door, then quickly pulled his head back.

"Hard to tell, but I think it's the same two guys," he hissed. Like street kids to the captain, paramilitaries all looked the same to Brodie.

Carlota took a quick look. "Oh God, it *is* them." She picked up a tomato and started slicing wildly, knocking a pile of yams to the floor with her elbow.

Brodie's eyelid started twitching madly. Try as he might, he couldn't control it.

Boots clumped on the deck as the paramilitaries approached. They were almost at the galley door when there was a shout and the blur of camouflage outfits rushing past. Then the sounds of a tussle and a cry of pain.

Brodie dared a peek. One of the paramilitaries had a deckhand in an armlock. The other clouted him with his rifle butt. The victim slumped senseless and they dragged him to the side and flung him into their boat. Then they followed and sped away.

"It's the new deckhand," Jorge, who was standing nearby, said. "They seemed to recognize him."

"What did he do?" asked Brodie.

Jorge shrugged. "Who knows? Maybe his family are guerrilla supporters – poor guy."

La Rosa's paddle wheel started up again, and the journey downriver continued.

The day wore on. Brodie, sweltering in the galley, pulled a greasy frying pan out of the dishwater and began scrubbing at it. He reached up blindly for a towel to wipe the sweat from his forehead. The towel was soaked through already and he tossed it aside and worked on, ignoring the rivulets of sweat running off him into the dishpan.

Just remember, he told himself, *in a few days we'll be in the mountains. They say it's cool up there. Nothing ordinary about this country – you can be sweltering down here one day, cool in the mountains the next. Nothing ordinary about the people either. Look at Father César – all the troubles he has, yet he took time to help us without giving it a second thought. And old Captain Alberto in the* hospedaje, *finding us this job even though he didn't know us from a hole in the ground. And Jorge and Great-aunt and Luis and Rafael . . . and most of all, Carlota. I've met more new friendly people here in one week than in my whole life.*

But then there are the others, he reminded himself, *like Don Antonio and Pablo. It doesn't take many of them to ruin it for everyone else.*

He slammed the frying pan down hard on the draining board, as if it were their skulls. *We'll show those guys,* he vowed. *We'll find my father, and when we do, we'll take him right out from under their noses.*

24

The backpacker picked them up in his rented jeep as they were trudging along the road from the coast. The jeep was loaded with gear — backpack, tent, bedroll, groceries, water — which he had to rearrange to make room for them.

They had wondered how they'd ever find their way when they first gazed up at the Sierra Nevada massif from the coast — that was after saying good-bye to Captain Alvarez and Jorge, and taking the bus from Barranquilla back to the Guajira Peninsula. Determined, Brodie had said, "We'll do it somehow," and they started walking down the dirt road that led inland.

From a distance the foothills appeared to come almost to the sea, but they soon discovered it was a long, long way when you were walking. They walked for hours and the mountains didn't seem any closer. *We're getting nowhere fast,* Brodie thought, trying to work up enough saliva to spit the dust out of his mouth. Then the jeep had braked to a stop beside them.

The backpacker in the jeep was an American, breezy and confident. "I love this country. It has everything," he said in his limited Spanish, which he filled in with English words and frequent gestures. "Just look at it – Cartagena and the Caribbean back there," he gestured behind him to the west, "the Sierra Nevadas up there (gesture ahead), the Guajira desert over there (gesture to the north), the Magdalena, the Andes, the jungle, Bogotá (sweeping gesture to the south)." The jeep swerved and Brodie wished the guy would keep his hands on the wheel. "All that, and generous, friendly people. I love it," the backpacker said.

He's right, Brodie thought, *it is a spectacular country.* He was tempted to talk to him in English but he resisted, wanting to keep his Colombian street kid identity. Just in case they met a paramilitary roadblock.

"Where you kids going?" the backpacker asked.

"Up there," Brodie said. He pointed to the mountains ahead.

The backpacker grinned. "Sorry, but I can't drive you up there. Just going to the end of the road to see the Indian village."

"How far is that?"

The backpacker didn't understand. Brodie had to repeat it slowly.

"Ah, how far? Fifteen miles or so."

"Are they Wayúu?" Carlota asked.

"Huh?"

"Are they Wayúu Indians?"

"Indians is all I know. The man who rents the jeeps told me." He downshifted as the road began to climb. "You really going up into those mountains?"

Brodie nodded.

"Where's your . . . you know." He pointed to his gear.

"We don't have any," said Brodie.

The backpacker shook his head. "You must be . . ." he searched for the Spanish word, gave up, and settled for "tough," said loudly in English. "It's cold up there at night, you know." He took his hands off the wheel to pantomime clutching himself and shivering. The jeep lurched toward the ditch. "And wet too," he added, grabbing the wheel back just in time.

The Indian village at the end of the road was not Wayúu. But it was, it turned out, the village of a related tribe. The Indians were distant at first, ignoring the visitors, but when Carlota spoke a few words of Wayúu to them, their demeanor changed instantly. They knew the village where her relatives lived and they remembered her great-aunt, Graciela. The village elder invited the three travelers into one of the circular wooden huts for a meal.

"I'm sure glad I picked you two up," the backpacker said, as he tucked into a bowl of fish, corn, and plantain. He'd given up trying to find the right words in Spanish once Brodie relented and admitted he understood a little English.

Afterwards, the Indians pointed out the route up the mountain and pressed food on Carlota, packed in a woven carryall.

"Are there paramilitary patrols?" she asked.

The old chief spat. "Paramilitary troublemakers, you mean. They were here last week. Hope they don't ever come back, but who knows."

"I'm worried about you with no shelter tonight," the backpacker said, as they were saying good-bye. "Tell you what, I'll lend you my spare pup tent. It's nylon, weighs practically nothing."

"Thank you for the offer, but how can we return it?" said Brodie.

The backpacker made a dismissive gesture. "Ah, don't worry about that. If you come back this way, give it to the man who rents the jeeps. He'll keep it for me."

Brodie shivered. The misty rain plastered his hair to his scalp, ran down his face and neck, and soaked his running shoes. They'd been climbing all afternoon, and his legs were aching and his ankle hurt where he'd turned it on a stone. The ankle slowed him down. Carlota stopped and waited for him to catch up. "Time for a break," she panted.

He sat on a rock by the side of the trail, massaging his ankle. A damp, earthy smell rose around him. Lush green growth was everywhere – trees, bushes, shrubs, vines, ferns – spurred on by the heavy rainfall. Thirteen feet a year of rain, the Indians in the village had told them. Matchless country for growing coffee – or marijuana when coffee prices plummeted.

Just above his head, a cluster of orchids clung to a mossy tree. A hummingbird poked its long thin beak into an orchid, drank, then darted to the next one.

He got to his feet reluctantly and they started climbing again. They kept going until the light began to fade.

"We'd better set up the tent," he suggested. "Be dark soon."

They couldn't find a clearing for it in the dense growth on either side and had to set it up on the trail itself, where it leveled out for a short way. They fell inside, wet and exhausted.

Carlota opened the woven bag the Indians had given them and the tent filled with the aroma of fried plantain. The food was wrapped in layers of sturdy green leaves and was still slightly warm. To Brodie it tasted like heaven.

Their two bodies, stretched out, filled the tent. They lay back-to-back, their body heat gradually warming each other. Brodie listened to the patter of rain on the tent. He could feel the muscles of Carlota's back pressing against his, and a sensation like an electric current flowed into him. He wondered if she felt it too. Whatever it was, the sensation somehow heightened his sense of being alive, so that, strangely, he found himself wishing they could stay like this – together in a cramped tent on the slope of a mountain in the rain – forever.

A sound outside woke him. He heard it again. A loud rustling noise in the bushes. *A puma? A jaguar?* The Indians had said they might see either. He lay there, his ears straining, and thought he heard sniffing – or was that his imagination? He wondered if he should throw the remains of the food in the bushes to distract whatever was there. But then it might come back, looking for more. He did nothing and the rustling stopped, but he didn't get back to sleep until it began to get light.

When he next awoke, Carlota was gone. He peered out through the tent flap. The rain had stopped. Clouds still hung on the mountain slope, but the sky was clearing. He scrambled out and stepped off the trail to relieve himself.

A pair of eyes stared at him from behind a bush. Startled, he backed away, dribbling on his jeans. Something streaked away in a flash of yellow. *The puma from last night.* It seemed as frightened of him as he was of it.

Carlota appeared on the other side of the trail. "Over here," she called. "There's a stream and a waterfall."

Brodie splashed icy water from the stream on his face. He cupped his hands and took a long drink. Finding clean water was no problem here. He told her about the yellow eyes, but he didn't mention the sounds in the night.

They ate sparingly from the remaining food, saving some for later, and started out again. Brodie's ankle hobbled him at first, but it gradually loosened up. They walked in silence, concentrating on the climb. The trail became steeper and they had to lean into it, bodies almost parallel to the path. Then they crested a ridge and stopped, awed.

Far above them, they could see where the forest gave out. Above the tree line was bare, craggy rock — ridges and ravines — ending in snow-covered peaks. Condors, mere black specks, circled high above them.

Below the ridge where they stood lay a valley swathed in mist. The trail dipped down into the mist, then appeared again on the other side of the valley. They started down. Brodie thought back to Rafael's map they had tried to memorize before it went up in flames. They should be getting close.

At that moment, a figure in olive fatigues stepped out from behind a boulder, pointing a Kalashnikov.

Carlota, in the lead, jumped.

25

Brodie said a silent prayer that they had stumbled on a guerrilla sentry, not a paramilitary. As he came closer, he saw the sentry was a girl about their age. "I have a letter for your *comandante*," he heard Carlota say. *A guerrilla then,* he thought, with relief.

"You! Stay there!" the girl ordered Brodie. She gestured with her gun. "And keep your hands where I can see them."

She turned back to Carlota. "Show me the letter."

Carlota reached down to the patch she had sewn on her jeans. She put a finger in an open corner and ripped the stitching. The letter from Rafael fell out.

The girl perused it carefully, still keeping an eye on them. When she finished, she looked from Carlota to Brodie and back again, as if trying to place them in the strange tale she had just read. Then she motioned. "Go ahead," she said.

She waited for them to pass, then followed close behind, calling out instructions where the trail branched.

Comandante Diego put down the letter. "It's good to hear from my friend Rafael again," he said. "I owe him a lot – perhaps he told you."

"No, he didn't, *Comandante*," Carlota said.

"Call me Diego. Everybody else does."

They were in the *comandante*'s tent. Brodie, sharing a crude bench – a board resting on two stumps – with Carlota, studied him. This was the person everything depended on. He had a scar on his cheek and sat in his camp chair with one leg stretched out stiffly in front of him, as if it wouldn't bend.

"Your brother," Diego went on, "saved my life. We were ambushed by a paramilitary troop and had to retreat. I took a bullet in the leg and collapsed. Rafael risked his neck to come back and get me." He looked at the letter again. "Still, it is a lot he is asking me to do – freeing his good friend, Señor Bailey."

"It is a lot to ask," Carlota admitted, "but there is nothing for you to gain by holding him. There is no ransom to be had. No one to pay."

"They all say that at first," Diego responded quietly. "But as the months – sometimes the years – go by, they begin to discover there is money after all. In the meantime, we do not harm the captive. We merely hold him, or her, and wait."

But what if there really is no ransom in the end? Brodie wondered. *Then what?*

"It is our way of taxing the wealthy for the good of our country," Diego continued. "The privileged class have to realize they must share their country's wealth with the poor. But they want to keep it all for themselves."

Brodie thought Diego was probably right about that. At the same time he was perplexed. All this fighting and killing and kidnapping, what did it accomplish? There had to be a better way to share the wealth of a country.

Diego finally got down to specifics. "I would do anything for Rafael. But this. . . ." He lifted his hands in a gesture of helplessness. "You see, we are keeping Señor Bailey under an arrangement with certain others who will share the ransom with us. If I had known he was a friend of Rafael's, I never would have agreed to it."

Brodie spoke up for the first time. "Perhaps you could convince the others that there really is no possibility of ransom in this case."

Diego turned to him. "I believe it when you say there is no money because I know Rafael would not send you here to deceive me. But the others will not believe it."

Brodie tried again. "But you have nothing to gain for all your trouble."

"Apparently not," Diego admitted. He looked thoughtful. "I wish I could let you take your father back with you, but unfortunately. . . ." He stood up. "Now I must attend to my duties."

"But can't you . . . ," Brodie began. Surely all their efforts weren't going to end here.

Diego wasn't listening. He ushered them out of the tent. "Give your brother my very best wishes," he said to Carlota. Turning to Brodie, he put his hand on his shoulder. "Don't despair, young man. One never knows what will happen next in this world."

Brodie watched him walk away. *What can he mean by that?*

He looked around the campsite desperately. He'd asked if he could see his father when they first arrived, but Diego said firmly that it was impossible. Maybe they could fake leaving, he thought, then double back and try to find where his father was. He could be close by.

But Diego instructed the sentry to escort them down the trail and see them on their way, so that was the end of that.

There was nothing else to do but go. Despondently, they followed the sentry.

26

"Don't despair," the *comandante* had told him. "One never knows what will happen next." Brodie kept turning that remark over in his mind. It was the only hopeful note they had come away with yesterday, and he clung to it like moss to a high mountain rock. Did it mean anything? Or had he merely said it to get rid of them?

They were on the road back to Santa Marta, wondering if they had missed the bus and would have to walk all the way. He was hot and frustrated. He guessed Carlota was feeling the same, for when he wasn't paying attention and weaved into her, she glared at him. *She's taking it as hard as I am,* he thought, *even though it was my father we failed to rescue.*

Every step seemed an effort now that they didn't have a goal ahead. Every step was taking them away from his father. Brodie thought wearily about the miles they'd already walked today – and yesterday, making their way down the mountain. Their Indian friends had seen how exhausted they were when they reached the village, and insisted they rest there for the night. Early this morning, they had said good-bye and set off on the dusty road to the sea. There was no backpacker in a jeep this time.

At a small town, they'd found the man who rented jeeps and left the backpacker's tent with him. The bus to Santa Marta, he told them, could be flagged down once they reached the coastal highway.

From Santa Marta they would catch the bus that went by Great-aunt's place. Brodie counted his money. He had just enough for the bus fares and to pay Great-aunt what he owed her.

"Here it comes," Carlota said at last. They flagged the bus down and squeezed aboard. Being a Sunday it was jammed with families coming back from the beach, with their picnic hampers and towels. There was standing room only. A jovial woman near them was offering the remains of her picnic all around. Brodie hung on to the overhead rail with one hand and ate homemade banana bread with the other. He began to feel back in the world.

They got off the second bus – the one they caught in Santa Marta – at Great-aunt's. The bus lurched away with a roar, which gradually faded. Brodie stood savoring the silence that followed, a relief after the hurly-burly of Santa Marta and the crowded buses. Carlota hurried ahead, down the dip in the path, anxious to see her great-aunt and uncles again. At the second rise, she stopped suddenly, staring ahead.

Brodie ran up to her. "What?"

She was staring at the burnt-out shell of a house.

"Oh, my God!" he said.

She turned and buried her face in his shoulder.

There was nothing left but ashes and the remnant of the fireplace with the cooking pots that had hung in it. Blackened remains of once-colorful pottery stuck out of the ashes. Brodie hoped Carlota wouldn't poke around, looking for familiar things. If she did, he was afraid she might find something awful.

"Paramilitaries," she hissed. Brodie remembered the man on the bus to Barranquilla – the one with the dark glasses who was staring at Great-aunt's disappearing back. "They have long memories," Great-aunt had said.

He glanced around the property. One shed was all that was standing. The door of the shed screeched as they opened it. Inside were tools, a shovel, a machete, and piled at the end, sacks of plantain, mangoes, rice, and bananas. *They couldn't take those with them when they fled,* Brodie thought. *If they did flee. If they hadn't been –*

"*Dios mío* – look!" Carlota said.

A rectangular mound of fresh earth lay not far from the shell of the house. At the head of the mound, someone had placed a rough cairn of rocks. There was no name on the cairn. Carlota stood looking down at the grave, her head bowed.

A bleating from the woods brought her head up sharply. "Enrique!" she cried, and ran to find him.

Brodie hurried to the shore. He stared across the bay to where they had left *Southern Cross*. All he could see was a solid wall of mangroves. His heart sank. *Has the boat gone too?* Then he caught a flash of white among the densely packed trees. *An egret?* Flocks of the pure white birds sometimes nested in the mangroves. *Or could it possibly be? . . .*

He plunged into the shallow water, knees pumping, spray flying. He tripped over a root and was sent sprawling. Up again in an instant, he plunged on until he reached the densest stand of mangroves, where he'd seen the flash of white. He wrenched aside the foliage.

Yes, there she is!

Southern Cross had been cleverly hidden. Someone – the uncles no doubt – had cut a channel into the very heart of the mangroves. *Must have taken days of work to hack through those tough roots,* he thought. They had hauled *Southern Cross* in and woven the cuttings behind her – a perfect screen.

Pushing aside branches, clambering over roots, he reached the stern. Even the dinghy was still there, calmly waiting for him.

Brodie suddenly had the feeling he was being watched. He looked around. Nothing. But the feeling wouldn't go away.

Someone had let down the swim ladder. He climbed up it.

"Bro*dee*," a voice said, "is that you?"

Eyes looked out at him from the dimness of the companionway. The eyes became a woman in a tattered purple-and-yellow dress as she emerged into the cockpit.

"Great-aunt!" he said, embracing her.

Behind her came one of the uncles – the one who had talked about how he would hide the boat for him. Luis.

Great-aunt was staring behind Brodie. "I'm afraid to ask. Carlota? Is she? . . ."

"She's fine," Brodie assured her. "She'll be so relieved to see you. Let's go tell her." He untied the dinghy.

Great-aunt hung back, which was unusual for her. "I don't think I can go there yet," she said. "Bring her here, Bro*dee*."

He rowed to the shore, calling to Carlota. By the time he was halfway there, she was wading out to meet him.

27

"They came in the night," Great-aunt said. "No one warned us this time." Her eyes had a sad faraway look. "That's the trouble with living among strangers."

"The grave?" Carlota asked. "Is it? . . ."

Great-aunt nodded, unable to speak the name. Her lips quivered.

Carlota hugged her.

"It's Manuel," Luis said. "The thatch went up so fast, he was unable to get out in time. They threw gasoline torches on the roof."

Great-aunt swallowed and took up the story. "Luis and I managed to slip out the back, seconds before the roof fell in. We hid in the woods. The next day we buried our brother and decided to leave this place forever. But Luis insisted we wait until you returned. He was worried about the boat."

Luis shrugged, smiling awkwardly. "We had promised to take care of it."

"Thank you," Brodie said. "You did a great job of hiding it."

"Will you go farther away this time, Great-aunt?" Carlota asked. "Somewhere you will be safer?"

"No," she said vehemently. "We are not going to run anymore. We are going home."

Home, Brodie thought. Till now it was just a word to him. Hearing Great-aunt, it suddenly had meaning. The place where you're not among strangers anymore.

"Back to the Guajira?" Carlota said. "But isn't that risky?"

"Pah! No more risky than this." Great-aunt gestured toward the burnt-out house and the grave. "In our Wayúu village, we will at least be among friends. But tell me about your journey. Did you find Rafael? And what about Bro*dee's* father?"

Carlota recounted their trip up the Magdalena, the meeting with Rafael, and their trek to deliver his letter. When she mentioned the Indian village in the foothills, Great-aunt nodded. "I know it well. So with the help of the villagers, you were able to find the guerrilla camp and free your father, Bro*dee?*"

"We found the camp," Brodie said. "But we didn't free my father. If it had been up to *Comandante* Diego, I think he would have released him after he read Rafael's letter. But he couldn't, he said, because there were others involved. We weren't even able to see my father."

Great-aunt touched Brodie's cheek sympathetically. "How hard for you – to be so close. What will you do now?"

He sighed. "If there was anything more I could do, I would. Carlota has been a terrific help, everybody has, but. . . ." He shrugged. "Just have to wait and hope for the best. I might as well go, I guess." *Go where?* he wondered.

He saw Carlota look at him sharply and tried to read her expression – disappointment that he was going? Or was that wishful thinking?

Great-aunt stood up. "Now that you are safely back, Luis and I will get ready to leave." She looked down at her smudged and torn dress. "I'll have to go like this – all my dresses were burned. The first thing I'll do when I get back to my village is make a new one."

"Will you take the bus?" asked Carlota.

"I wish we could. But we have to take Enrique with us, and the food and tools from the shed. My cousins have a truck, but it broke down. If they can't fix it, they will come for us with their cart and donkey."

"It's a long way to the Guajira on a donkey cart – it will take forever," said Carlota.

Great-aunt shrugged.

Something clicked in Brodie's mind. "I have a better idea," he said. "We'll take you in the boat. We can take everything easily – even Enrique." *Am I ready to go through that again?* he wondered. "It will be much faster for you. Two days at the most and we'll be there."

"That is very kind of you," Great-aunt said, "but. . . ."

She glanced around the cabin apprehensively, as if picturing water pouring in through the hull. "I have a great fear of the ocean. A seer told me once that the ocean would take someone close to me."

"You'll be quite safe – Bro*dee* is an excellent sailor," Carlota said. "You must come. It will be much easier for you."

"All right, but I'll spend all my time in the cabin with my eyes squeezed shut," Great-aunt said.

Brodie was pleased. He had been dreading the thought of sailing away from Carlota. Yet he knew the time had to come. She had her own plans. At least he would be with her a few more days.

They decided to leave first thing in the morning. They rowed the supplies and tools from the shed out to the boat and distributed the weight of the heavy sacks evenly – some in the bow V-berth, some amidships, some in the stern locker. Luis waded into the mangroves to clear away the brush, and they pulled *Southern Cross* out of her hiding place with the dinghy. Then, while Brodie and Carlota uncovered the sails and made ready, Great-aunt cooked dinner – a delicious concoction of leftover canned food from the boat's cupboards and rice, plantains, and spices from her food sacks.

That night, Brodie and Carlota slept on the deck on cushions, leaving the cabin to Great-aunt and Luis. Brodie lay awake, swatting at mosquitoes and wondering what to do after this short trip was over.

It was now, it seemed, a matter of waiting — who knows how long — and hoping for his father's release. He shifted restlessly. Where should he go? The thought of sailing away left a great emptiness inside him.

He thought about Great-aunt's desire to go home. At least she knew where home was. He pictured the places he'd lived in his short life. Ottawa, Florida with his mother, on the boat with his father. The only one of those that had felt at all like home was Ottawa. But there was nothing for him there now. *So where is home? Everyone has some place that feels like home, don't they?*

The only place he could think of, strangely enough, was right here in Colombia. Funny, after this short time, that he would feel so at home here. Maybe it had something to do with Carlota.

He shifted over until his face was close to hers, watching her long eyelashes flicker as in a dream. *And what about the two of us?* he wondered. He found it easy to say he loved Colombia — even the backpacker in the jeep could say that — but it was much harder to say he loved Carlota. For one thing, he wasn't sure what it meant. How do you know if you love someone? He had no idea. All he knew was he wanted to be with her. *But she's so different from me,* he thought. *She knows exactly where she's going; I'm just drifting.*

He fell asleep, still with no idea what he would do, or what, if anything, would come next for them.

28

Robert Bailey slumped against the tent pole. He scratched at the growth on his chin. It was getting more scraggly every day and it itched. He wished he could shave it off, but they wouldn't allow him a razor. He hitched up his pants, which were slipping down over his hips. He had been thin to start with and he'd lost a lot of weight. Not that they didn't feed him, but sometimes only once a day, and the food always the same – yucca and plantain and beans. Cooped up, depressed, he had little appetite for it.

Gradually, too, he was losing hope. He knew there was no one to help him – except Brodie, and there wasn't much Brodie could do. Robert had deliberately cut himself off from everyone who cared about him and now he was paying for it. If he ever did get out of there alive, he vowed he would no longer be the loner he'd become. It was a tough world out there, he realized now, tougher than he'd ever imagined, and a man needed friends.

He played a game to pass the time, imagining what he'd do if, by some miracle, he was freed. He pictured himself returning home, renewing friendships. Even swallowing his pride and getting back into the world of the civil service he knew so well. Brodie would be disappointed, he thought, but he's young and could sail to the Pacific some other time.

He shuffled to the entrance of the small tent and peered out. The guard was still lounging against a tree, where he could watch both tents. Robert knew they hadn't given them separate tents out of the goodness of their hearts. It must have been because they didn't want them plotting an escape together. He didn't even know who was in the other tent. Sometimes he caught a glimpse of a shaggy-haired, unkempt figure who looked like he'd been there a long time.

They were taken out separately to empty the pails that served as their toilets. At first that was often for Robert, as he'd developed amebic dysentery. Lately the dysentery had faded. *Thank God for small mercies,* he thought.

A man the guard called *Comandante* appeared every day or two and grilled him. He demanded details of Robert's bank accounts and property, and the names of business associates. Robert kept telling him the same thing: little money of his own and no business associates left. Sometimes the *comandante* became incensed and called him a liar. "You'll change your mind when you've been here a year," he would growl.

At least he didn't slap him around, like the other one – the little guy from the trawler. He was the one who had brought him here from town on that long miserable march Robert thought would never end. He'd been taken from the house blindfolded and thrown into a truck. Then he was led, stumbling, up the mountain on a rope, like a donkey. All he could tell was that they were going up, and that it got wetter and colder as they climbed.

The little guy's idea of interrogation had been to clout him whenever Robert gave an answer he didn't like. He still had the bruises, and the cigarette burns on his arms. The second day in the house, Robert had heard him talking about *el yate* with the tall one. He knew then that they had connected him to the foreign yacht in the harbor. "We'll take his yacht, and our share of the ransom, too," he'd heard them say.

He worried constantly about Brodie. If *Southern Cross* was seized, what would happen to him? *Brodie would be helpless against these guys,* he thought.

Now, at the tent door, he examined the sky. The rain of the past few days had stopped and it was beginning to clear. That was a relief – his tent leaked badly and everything he touched was soggy.

When the sun appeared, he took careful note of its position. By watching its progress, he would be able to tell which way was west. To the west would be the coast – if he ever got out of here.

He felt better once he figured that out. If he did get a chance to escape, at least he would know which way to

head. Not that he was ever likely to get the chance. There was always a guard.

The first time the *comandante* came, he warned Robert against trying to escape. He'd perish in the mountains before he found his way out, he said. Still, they didn't take any chances. At night, or if the guard had other duties during the day, they shackled his ankles.

Now, as Robert watched, the guard suddenly scrambled to his feet and doused his cigarette. A few minutes later, the *comandante* strode into the clearing. Another grilling, Robert assumed.

The *comandante* ducked through the tent flap and stood, hands on hips, looking at him. "You should be proud to have a son like that," he said.

Robert waited. *What does he mean?*

"He not only found out where you are," the *comandante* went on, "he climbed all the way up here to plead your case."

Robert was stunned.

"Unfortunately, I had to tell him I could not let you go. Others are involved, as you know. They would be very angry if I freed you."

"Is he all right?" Robert asked anxiously. "What have you done with him?"

"He's gone back. A bit discouraged, understandably, after all his efforts."

He risked his life for me, Robert thought.

"Of course, I can't let you go just because I admire

your son's effort. On the other hand. . . ." He rubbed his chin. "They were smart, bringing me that letter from Rafael. They knew what they were doing."

Now what's he saying? Robert wondered. The *comandante* seemed to be arguing with himself. He sat on the upturned pail, his chin on his hand. Which was unusual, Robert thought — he'd always stood over him before, as if to emphasize his dominant position.

"How was I to know you were an old family friend?" he said. He was staring at Robert, yet seemed to be looking right through him. "I would do anything in my power for Rafael. But this isn't in my power. . . ." He sat up suddenly. "Or is it? Of course I can't free you just like that. However, if you were to escape. . . . Yes, that would be different. It happens. When we launch a raid on a government target or change campsites, it takes our attention away from our prisoners. There have been escapes before. The others would have to accept it, that's all."

Robert was confused. *Who is this Rafael?* he wondered. *What is this about an old family friend?* Still the very fact he had used the word "escape" — in fact, almost seemed to be offering it as a possibility — was enough to make his pulse leap.

"Yes, they would just have to accept it, wouldn't they?" the *comandante* said again. Then he got to his feet abruptly and strode from the tent, as if he had made up his mind about something.

While Robert was still pondering the significance of all this, he heard the *comandante* call out an order. Scrambling to the entrance, he watched the guard head for the second tent, returning moments later with the other captive. The guard then took the handcuffs from his belt and started back toward Robert's tent.

Robert assumed he was coming to shackle him as usual while they went off somewhere. But the *comandante* barked out a second order and the guard stopped. Looking puzzled, he shrugged and put the handcuffs away. Then, shepherding the other captive, he followed the *comandante* down the trail.

Robert watched in disbelief as they disappeared. He was left alone. Alone and unshackled.

He waited. Was it some kind of trick? Were they encouraging him to try to escape as an excuse to shoot him? Get rid of him because there was no ransom money? He edged out of the tent, walked cautiously to the edge of the clearing, and stared down the trail.

Narrow and girdled by bush, it was like looking into the mouth of a tunnel. He listened for voices. A bird sang a few notes, otherwise there was silence. Perhaps someone would come laboring up the trail at any minute. Perhaps a replacement guard sent from the main camp below.

No one came.

Robert took a few tentative steps. It was chancy; a shot might ring out from a hidden guard. But anything was better than being held there for years, he decided. He started cautiously down the trail.

Maybe Brodie has really done it! he thought. And he'd always treated him like he was just an inept kid.

29

They sailed north to clear the land, then turned east toward the Guajira Peninsula. Brodie still had to navigate by eye, thanks to Enrique and his appetite for paper. The goat stood placidly behind him in the cockpit, content as long as Carlota was with him. Great-aunt hadn't ventured out of the saloon, but Luis was up on the deck, feet apart, holding on and watching the sea roll by.

Until Brodie made the turn to the east, the sailing had been easy, sheltered by the jutting coastline. But now the east wind and the current were both dead against them. Luis retreated to the cockpit as spray began to sweep across the deck.

"I'll head out to sea and stay well away from the shore," Brodie told him, "until we reach Riohacha." Riohacha was the port on the Guajira Peninsula closest to Luis and Great-aunt's village. With no chart to plot his progress, he'd have to guess at his course. As he remembered, Riohacha was about a hundred miles to the east. Against the wind and current they'd be lucky to make three or four knots, so that would mean tomorrow morning.

They were past Santa Marta and the worry of avoiding the freighters heading in and out of the busy port. Now there was only the occasional one to watch out for – a coal boat heading for the Guajira to pick up a load, or a *contrabandista* heading the same way.

A small freighter was coming up behind them now. Brodie altered course to keep clear, muttering to himself as he did. According to the rules, the overtaking craft was supposed to keep clear. But when a freighter that could plow you under was speeding up behind, he judged it best to stay well out of the way.

The freighter charged past, engines throbbing, the helmsman staring at them. Brodie remembered his last encounter with a freighter here. That was the time the man on the bridge had watched them through binoculars, and Carlota had suspected he was a *narco* radioing information about the foreign yacht. He hoped this wasn't another freighter with *narcos* aboard, friendly to Don Antonio.

"Take over and I'll go see how Great-aunt is doing," he said to Carlota.

He found her sitting bolt upright, clutching a post. "Is everything all right?" she asked. "It feels like we're tipping over."

Brodie assured her it was normal for a sailboat to lean. "But it will be rough all the way, I'm afraid," he said. He saw she was looking pale. "You might feel better in the fresh air."

"You're sure it's safe to come up?"

"I'm sure."

She stood up. "Then I'll try it."

After she'd been with them in the cockpit for a while, Brodie noticed Great-aunt was beginning to relax. She sat watching the shore fading away, with the Sierra Nevadas in the distance. They made steady progress for the rest of the day.

It was late afternoon when Brodie first spotted the vessel coming towards them from the direction of the coast. All he could see was the top of its wheelhouse. He stared as it appeared and disappeared between swells, and a chill swept through him.

It's a trawler, but is it that *trawler? Has the word been passed along from the freighter? Has* Southern Cross *been tracked all the way?*

If it was the trawler, there was absolutely nothing he could do. No way he could evade it in daylight, unless a storm came to shield them. He searched the sky. Only small white puffs of cloud, and the usual fringe around the distant mountains. No help there.

"Better go below," he said to Great-aunt and Luis. He wanted them out of harm's way, but he didn't want to alarm them. "I need room in the cockpit to maneuver."

As the trawler closed in, he heard Carlota gasp. "Oh no, it's them!"

The trawler cut across their bow. So close he had only two choices: ram it or turn into the wind and stall. For a second he considered ramming. Then he pictured a gaping hole in *Southern Cross*'s bow. He turned into the wind.

The trawler wheeled and tried to come alongside. But with both boats being tossed about in the heavy sea, the trawler had to keep its distance to avoid a collision. Brodie had room to swing off the wind. The sails filled again and *Southern Cross* picked up speed. The two boats raced along side by side.

Staring at them across twenty feet of heaving sea was Don Antonio. Beside him was the little guy, Pablo, his weasel-like features set in a smirk. He was holding a rifle.

Don Antonio called across the gap, "Drop your sails."

Brodie hesitated. Pablo raised the gun. "Better do it," Carlota said. She took over the wheel while he let the sheets go and rolled in the jib, his mind a turmoil. This time there was no way out. Why did he ever suggest taking Great-aunt and Luis home! Instead of helping, he'd led them all into a trap.

He released the halyard, and yanked down the main. *Southern Cross* drifted to a stop and sat heaving in the swells. The trawler slowed to stay alongside.

Stalling, Brodie gathered up the sail and began folding it along the boom.

"Hurry up," Pablo shouted. They were drifting apart.

Don Antonio looked up at the wheelhouse and said something. The helmsman, Brodie saw, was Don

Antonio's son, Alfredo. He circled and maneuvered the trawler in closer.

"Who's in the cabin?" Don Antonio called.

Brodie pretended he didn't hear.

Don Antonio pointed at the binoculars hanging around his neck. "I saw four of you. Tell them to come out. Quickly, before I lose my patience."

Great-aunt's head emerged. She climbed up the companionway and glared across at Don Antonio.

He was clearly taken aback. For a long moment, he and Great-aunt stared at each other across the thrashing cauldron of water. Don Antonio was the first to drop his gaze.

A wave tossed the trawler closer. Brodie shouted a warning: "Watch out – you'll stave us in." He reached for the starter button to get out of the way.

"Don't move!" Pablo shouted. He leveled his gun at Brodie.

"We're wasting time," Brodie heard him say to Don Antonio. "The boat is ours. Let's get it over with."

He froze. He'd heard that was what narcos did when they took over a yacht – dump the occupants overboard. They were never seen again – no witnesses to report to the coast guard.

"You can have the boat," Brodie called. "Get rid of me, but take the others to shore. They have nothing to do with this."

Pablo snorted derisively. His finger tightened on the trigger.

Don Antonio put out a restraining hand. "A moment, Pablo." He looked across at Great-aunt. "I am sorry, Graciela. But I have to do what I have to do." He raised his voice over the noise of the trawler's engine. "I must have the yacht as compensation. Those careless guerrillas may have let the gringo get away, but I cannot settle for nothing. My reputation would suffer." He staggered and grabbed the rail as a wave rocked the trawler. "In this business, your reputation is everything." His gaze hardened. "The whole Guajira Peninsula has to know that no one gets the better of Don Antonio. Ever."

"Don Antonio, I —" Great-aunt began.

He held up his hand. "I particularly regret that you have somehow become involved in this. I never thought that I would have to do this to *you*."

"I am old. What happens to me is of little importance," Great-aunt said. "But I beg you, let the young ones go."

Don Antonio shook his head. "I can't leave any witnesses — especially not the young gringo." He sighed. "I regret this whole business. I never would have gotten involved if these idiots," he gestured scornfully at Alfredo and Pablo, "had left the planning to me. Had I been on board that morning, I would have let Señor Bailey stay in the sea to drown." He lifted his arms and dropped them in resignation. "But now I have to salvage what I can from this sorry affair." He nodded at Pablo, then he turned his back.

"Line up on the rail," Pablo ordered.

No one moved. A shot rang out. Brodie heard the buzz of a bullet close to his ear.

"Quickly!" Pablo said.

They shuffled onto the deck. Enrique tried to follow Carlota, but was restrained by his halter, which she had looped around the compass stand.

They stood in a line along the rail, mutely facing Pablo's gun. A feeling of helplessness swept through Brodie. What had he done, leading those he cared for into this? He gazed at Carlota, standing erect beside him, and his hand moved blindly, seeking hers. She felt his touch and locked her fingers with his.

He had scarcely been able to take in the news that his father had escaped. *One of us made it anyway,* he thought. Small consolation when you and your love were doomed — yes, he did love her he realized now. *Is this how you know? Do you have to die to find out?* He took in her face one last time, the long eyelashes cast down, the expression sad, never again to transform into that fleeting smile.

On the other side of him, Great-aunt and Luis stood stoically. *They've seen so much. Been expecting something like this half their life.*

Pablo took aim. His gun pointed at Great-aunt. Brodie heard Carlota gasp. He squeezed her hand tighter and closed his eyes as the shot rang out.

When he opened them again, Great-aunt was still standing. She was staring at the trawler where Pablo was slumped across the rail. The rifle slipped from his grip and fell into the sea. Then he slowly toppled over the rail and followed it.

On the wheelhouse deck, a gun in his hand, stood Alfredo.

"You fool," Don Antonio cried, looking up.

Alfredo looked steadily back at him. "Do you think I wouldn't care if he shot my mother?"

"Your mother!" Don Antonio scoffed. "You don't believe those rumors, do you?"

"I wondered enough that I went to see her," Alfredo said. "She told me the truth, which is more than you ever did."

"Put that gun away, Alfredo," Don Antonio barked. "Show some sense for once."

Alfredo continued as if he hadn't heard. "She said it broke her heart, but she gave me up so I would have the advantages you could provide. . . ." A gust of wind swept his words away.

They heard only bits of what Alfredo was saying, like a shortwave broadcast fading in and out.

". . . she said you weren't a bad man, just confused about what was important."

Don Antonio flapped his arms in exasperation. ". . . may have been a bit harsh, but we can straighten things out between us . . . put that gun away."

"I've taken my last order from you."

"You'll regret this."

"Ah, now come the threats . . . know you won't rest until you get vengeance . . . I should shoot you now while I can . . . say it was an accident, make up a story . . . stalled engine, rogue wave, you and Pablo washed overboard . . . that's what *you* would do."

Staring across at this tableau, they watched transfixed as Alfredo lifted his gun and aimed it at Don Antonio's heart. The breeze died suddenly, as if Nature, too, was waiting in suspense, and they heard his next words clearly.

"But it's still my father I see in my sights," he said. "I can't." He lowered the gun and gestured with it. "Now get over to the rail and be ready to jump aboard the yacht when I say."

He went back into the wheelhouse and skillfully jockeyed the trawler back and forth to close in on *Southern Cross*. Don Antonio made one try for the ladder leading up, but Alfredo quickly stepped out with the gun. "Don't tempt me," he said, and his father retreated to the rail. The trawler edged in closer.

Brodie watched nervously as a wave lifted the bigger vessel high above them. It plunged down, a mere two feet separating its rude bulging side from the delicate hull of *Southern Cross*. "Now!" Alfredo shouted.

Don Antonio heaved his bulk across. One foot landed on the toe rail of the yacht. He made a grab for the lifeline, missed, and teetered backwards. The sea, thrashing wildly in the gap between the boats, reached up for him.

Great-aunt, closest to him, hesitated. Then, reaching out, she grasped his arm and pulled him in. He fell onto the deck beside her.

"Give me a day's head start before you let him ashore," Alfredo shouted. He laughed. "Maybe I'll go join the guerrillas." Then he saluted Great-aunt, and the trawler pulled away.

Great-aunt, none too gently, led a shaken Don Antonio below. "I should have let you fall into the sea," she said. "But, like our son, I couldn't do it."

30

D on Antonio sat hunched in a corner of the saloon. He looked diminished in size, like a deflated balloon. "My own son," he muttered over and over. "To do this to me." The others did their best to ignore him.

Carlota was at the wheel, Brodie at her side. In fact, he hadn't left her side since they'd set sail again. *Me and Enrique,* he thought. The goat was squeezed in between them, his chin on her arm, as if he knew he'd nearly lost her.

"I've been thinking," Brodie said, "we should dump Don Antonio off where it will do his reputation the most harm – wherever that is."

Carlota knew instantly. "Where we're going – Riohacha. It's the center of the Guajira, a busy place; he'll be seen all right."

"Maybe we should row him around the harbor first, like the British Navy used to do," Brodie said. "Too bad we can't flog him at the same time."

"He'll suffer in his own way." It was Great-aunt who

had come up from below. "News of how Alfredo humiliated him will spread quickly, believe me."

She held out a small bundle wrapped in a tea towel. "Here's all the knives in the galley. Hide them somewhere, just to be safe. Doubt he'll try anything, but Luis is watching him anyway."

Brodie took the bundle, lifted the lid of the bench seat, and tucked it under a jumble of mooring lines.

"I kept one," Great-aunt said, indicating the hem of her long dress. She smiled. "Just to chop vegetables for dinner, of course."

Brodie fiddled with the jib, pulling it in a bit, then letting it out. "I'm sorry, Great-aunt, that I put all of you in such danger. I should have known better."

She came over and hugged him. "Oh, Bro*dee*, it wasn't your fault."

Carlota reached out and squeezed Brodie's arm.

"You know," Great-aunt said, "I've always felt Antonio and I had unfinished business. And it turned out for the best. I'm proud of my son."

The next morning they were somewhere off the coast of the Guajira Peninsula. Just where, Brodie wasn't sure. He'd estimated the distance and direction they traveled through the night, but he had no chart to plot it on. As they closed in on the land, he saw white beaches, a harbor, and a large town to the south. *Riohacha?*

He called down to Great-aunt. She balanced in the cockpit, one hand on the compass stand for support, and surveyed the roofs of the town.

"Yes, that's it," she said. "See, there's the cathedral."

Brodie was buoyed by the thought that his dead reckoning had been almost perfect. He headed for the harbor.

Brodie and Carlota sat in the cockpit, watching the afternoon sun color the desert gold. They were alone. They had rowed Don Antonio to the wharf, where he had climbed out and slunk away. Great-aunt located her cousins at the market and they had come to the dock with their donkey cart for her supplies.

They happened to mention to Great-aunt that they had heard about a *norteamericano* who'd stumbled out of the forest and sought shelter in the Indian village in the foothills. Great-aunt immediately thought of Brodie's father and was able to find out that it was indeed a Señor Bailey.

"Yes!" Brodie said, punching the air with a fist. "That's great news."

"I'll send word you are here," Great-aunt said.

Later, their supplies loaded and Enrique tied behind, Great-aunt and Luis climbed aboard the cart. They continued to wave until it lumbered out of sight. Even Enrique kept looking back until they rounded a bend.

And now, Brodie wondered, *now what?* Again last night he'd gone over and over the same question. He knew only one thing for sure: after facing Pablo's gun, expecting to die, something had changed in him.

And what about Carlota and me?

Carlota must have been wondering the same thing. She turned to him. "Have you decided where you will go, Bro*dee?* After your father returns?"

He deflected the question, stalling. "Not sure. And you? Still thinking about law school?"

"More than ever, especially after being in Barranca and hearing Father César's stories." She stared at the mountains, lit by the sun. "There's so much I could do . . . so many people who need help. But first I have to get busy and make some money for university."

"Did you have good grades in high school?"

"Well, yes," she said, modestly.

"Top of the class?"

She nodded. "Skipped a couple of grades along the way."

"Maybe you could get a scholarship, then." *She's way ahead of me. I'd better get busy if I ever hope to catch up.*

"A scholarship . . . in Colombia?" She gave a wry smile. "No, I'm on my own. And what about you? Still going to sail across the Pacific?"

He looked around the cockpit – at the winches, the self-steering vane, the halyards, the sheets, the blocks – at all the familiar things he'd learned to master single-handed. It was an exhilarating feeling when *Southern Cross* was charging along under his control, all sails pulling. Maybe someday he would sail the Pacific, but not now. There were other things tugging at him now.

He shrugged. "I don't think so. Not sure where I'll go." He fiddled with the end of a line, tying and untying the same knot over and over. "I envy you, knowing exactly what you want to do."

"It's what I have to do," she said.

He sensed the passion in her voice. How much longer could he keep drifting? Running away, really. For he saw now that was what he'd been doing – running away. From what? From himself? From taking on responsibilities? From fear of failing?

"Still going to Cartagena to sing with the street musicians?" he asked.

She nodded. "This is the time to make money – tourist season." They watched a pelican plunge into the sea and emerge with the tail of a fish dangling from its pouch. "In fact, I might as well get going. Your father will be here any day."

"I guess," he said.

She stood up abruptly. "At least I don't have anything to pack," she said, making light of her departure, although he thought he noticed a slight catch in her voice. "I'll hop a bus to Santa Marta. Get that far today, anyway. Will you row me in?"

"Yeah . . . sure. Do you have the fare?"

"Great-aunt lent me enough to get there. Let's go."

Later, Brodie sat in the cockpit, staring at the wharf, missing her already. Why did he have to act so cool? He and his father could have taken her to Cartagena in the boat. He should have held her hands in his, looked into those beautiful brown eyes, and begged her to stay. Now he didn't even know how to get in touch.

Who am I kidding? he thought, in the next breath. *She's independent. She doesn't need a drifter like me.* She had walked away without a backward glance.

He watched a boy on the dock peddling the late edition of *El Tiempo,* shouting the headlines. Something about the kidnapping of a government minister. *There's a drama every day here. So many stories.*

Suddenly he leaped up, almost banging his head on the boom. *So many stories — maybe that's the answer! Write about them. Try to make sense of them.* That would be something he'd really like.

He paced, thinking furiously, and the more he thought the more excited he became. His mind raced. It would mean finishing high school first. His mother would like that. He could do it. Buckle down, work hard. He could take extra courses, finish high school in a year, enroll in journalism at a Florida college. Then come back here and find a job with a newspaper. Begin at the bottom, whatever he had to do to get started. He spoke Spanish, he liked to write, he really loved the Colombian people. Find a way to tell their stories — the good, the bad, the heroic. . . .

Then he had another idea. He could take journalism in Bogotá instead — at the same university Carlota would be going to. That would polish up his Spanish and he could be with her.

He paused. *Wait a minute, Brodie. You're taking too much for granted again. She has her own friends; she won't want you hanging around all the time.*

He paced round and round the cockpit. *Okay, so she won't. At least I know what I want to do now. I'll get going on it right away.* He brightened. *And I'll see her now and then at the university.*

He went below and rooted around until he found a pen and paper. Then he began a letter to his mother. *The first step in my new career,* he thought. He laughed out loud. *Career — never thought that word would apply to me.*

"What are you laughing at?"

Startled, he looked up. She was standing in the companionway, soaking wet from the swim.

"How about a ride to Cartagena?" he said. "Please."

Then they both began to laugh.

Epilogue

"You're not disappointed then, Dad?" Brodie said. "I was afraid you would be." He inched the wheel to starboard to take advantage of a wind shift.

His father had just come up from below with a plate of cheese and crackers balanced on a mug of tea. He smiled. "About sailing to the Pacific, you mean? No, in fact, I thought *you* would be the disappointed one." He sat down on the cockpit bench. "Funny, isn't it? We both had the same idea at the same time – get back where we belong."

Like that Beatles' song from Dad's era, Brodie thought. *"Get Back."* But it was going to take a while for him to get back. Because where he belonged, he knew now, was back in Colombia with Carlota, studying journalism.

They were on their way north after dropping Carlota off at Cartagena. Their route would take them through

the Windward Passage, between Cuba and Haiti, to the
Bahamas and on to Florida. There they would separate —
his father to store the boat before taking a plane back to
Ottawa, Brodie to move in temporarily with his mother.
He'd been happy to hear she was playing the piano again.
Her voice had sounded brighter on the phone.

"Can you really get your job back, Dad?" he asked.
The uncivil service, his father had called it, among other
things, when he lost his job.

"Not the same one as before," his father said. "But
I'll get something. I still have contacts. And after what
we went through, anything will feel good." He reclined
on the cockpit bench, blew on his tea, and took a sip.
"I liked your friend, Carlota. But are you sure about
going back there, Brodie? Myself, I never want to see
Colombia again."

"I'm sure," Brodie said. In fact, he couldn't wait. It
had been painful saying good-bye to Carlota. He'd
watched as she walked away, turning and waving, getting
smaller and smaller until she disappeared in a crowd of
tourists.

A squall raced across the water toward them, churn-
ing up the sea. Behind the heavy black cloud, however,
he saw that the sky was still blue. Looked like the squall
would be fierce, but brief.

"Squall coming," he warned.

His father examined the sky. "Nasty," he said. He set
down his cup and got up. "I'd better take the wheel."

"No, I can handle it, Dad," Brodie said. "You just relax."

The End

ACKNOWLEDGMENTS

My thanks to the many people who helped during the writing of this book. Special thanks to César Patarroyo and Daniel and Remedios Contreras, Colombians now living in Canada, and to Faye Tiessen; also to Helena for many hours of critiquing drafts, and to Sue Tate for wise editorial comments that helped shape this story.